Ranger Rick's®
STORYBOOK

RANGER RICK
NATIONAL WILDLIFE FEDERATION

Favorite Nature Tales from
Ranger Rick Magazine

# Ranger Rick's STORYBOOK

## Favorite Nature Tales from Ranger Rick Magazine

**Rhonda Lucas Donald**

Illustrated by

**Parker Jacobs**

muddy boots™

we jump in puddles

GUILFORD, CONNECTICUT

The National Wildlife Federation & Ranger Rick contributors: Children's
Publication Staff, Licensing Staff and National Wildlife Federation's
in-house naturalist, David Mizejewski. Thank you for joining National
Wildlife Federation and Muddy Boots in preserving endangered animals
and protecting vital wildlife habitats. The National Wildlife Federation is
a voice for wildlife protection, dedicated to preserving America's
outdoor traditions and inspiring generations of conservationists.

Published by Muddy Boots
An imprint of The Rowman & Littlefield Publishing Group, Inc.
4501 Forbes Blvd., Ste. 200
Lanham, MD 20706

www.rowman.com
MuddyBootsBooks.com

Distributed by NATIONAL BOOK NETWORK

British Library Cataloguing-in-Publication Information available
Library of Congress Control Number: 2018943000

ISBN 978-1-63076-214-8 (hardcover)
ISBN 978-1-63076-215-5 (e-book)

Printed in Malaysia, 2018

# Contents

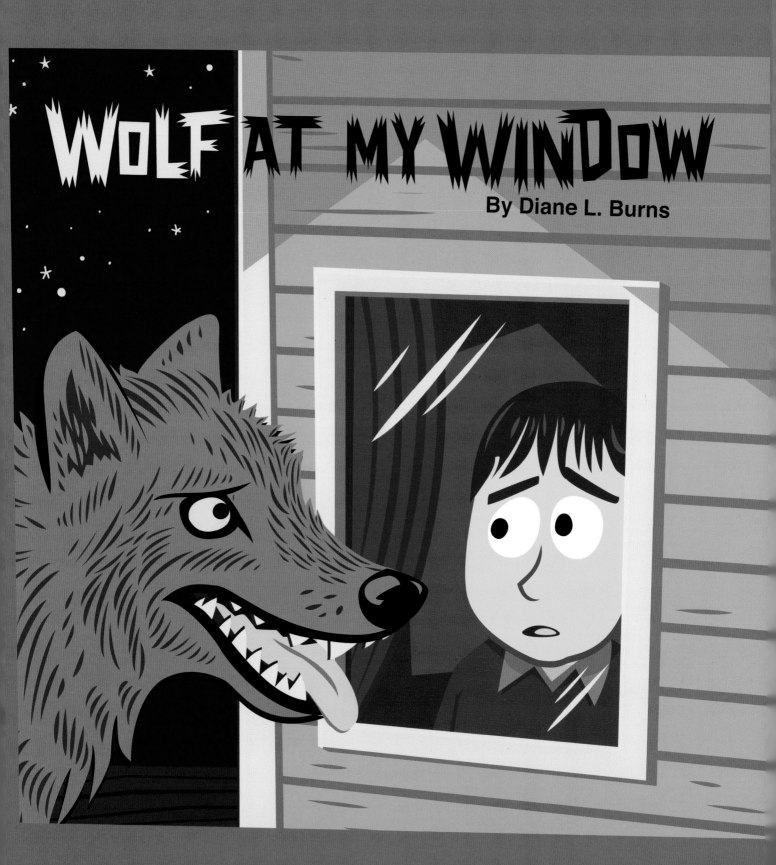

# WOLF AT MY WINDOW

By Diane L. Burns

*Wolf!* Matt was startled even to think the word. The boy stared out the cabin window at the lone creature. It was sitting a stone's throw away in the moonlight. The wolf howled; Matt shivered. For the first time, he felt truly alone in these Idaho mountains.

It had felt so good to be allowed to come along with Dad. Dad was a scientist who studied wild animals. Together, Matt and Dad had followed the tracks of mountain sheep, goats, and cougars. Through binoculars, they'd studied coyotes and mule deer. And they'd carefully recorded all the information in Dad's laptop every night in their tent. Dad would share the information with other wildlife scientists.

Then, two days ago, they had moved into an empty cabin. Here, Dad would write a report about what he had found. But they discovered that dozens and dozens of mice had taken over the cabin. The little rodents scurried in and out through tiny holes in the walls. Matt and his dad spent hours stuffing newspaper into all the holes they could find. But the mice just kept finding other holes—or making more.

Outside, underneath the window, crisscrossing mouse trails made patterns in the dried meadow grass. Inside, the mice had gotten into everything: the cupboards, Matt's jeans and boots, and even his pillow. Worst of all, the mice had gotten into the food and ruined almost everything.

Now, because most of the food was gone, Dad had left overnight to get new supplies from town. Matt had insisted on staying behind. "Don't you need someone to watch for whatever animals might come to the meadow?" he had asked his dad. Matt had expected to see a few mule deer—and to prove to himself that he could do just fine alone. He hadn't expected this wolf.

The wolf. Its howl sounded again. Matt opened the laptop to write about it, but his hands shook. Dad had never mentioned having any trouble with wolves. But Matt's friend Jill had once told him of a shopkeeper in Montana who'd faced a whole pack of wolves during a hard winter long ago. He'd been alone in his cabin, Jill had said.

*Like I am now,* Matt thought with a nervous gulp. The wolves had chewed right through a solid door, Jill had said, to get a smoked ham hanging from the ceiling.

But ... Matt took a deep breath and forced down his fright. How could such a story be true? Dad had told him many times that wolves were smart but shy, usually staying many miles away from people. The big, bad wolf was just a fairy tale, Matt thought. A 13-year-old boy was too old for such things.

Matt closed the computer and put it on the table. He glanced around for something he could use as a weapon—just in case. He grabbed a poker from the fireplace, went to the door, and took a deep breath. Then he opened the door, waved the poker, and yelled with all his might: "Go away, wolf! Go away!"

Startled, the wolf sprang up—and started trotting away. Matt closed the door and leaned back with a gasp. When he'd caught his breath, he turned back to the window. Oh, no! There was the wolf, sitting right where it had sat before.

Matt stared at the wolf. The wolf stared right back at him. Matt was staring into the eyes of a hunter, he knew. Like all creatures, the wolf needed to eat. Matt's dad had said that wolves play their part in the environment by eating deer, elk, rabbits, and other animals. But maybe, like the hungry mice that were frisking about Matt's feet, wolves go for any food they can find.

Then the wolf sprang! Matt ducked, expecting to hear the window glass shattering above him. Instead, he heard a muffled snuffling along the ground outside. The wolf wanted a way in! Matt shuddered. His heart pounded. If only Dad were here!

Now came a scratching sound—the sound of pawing at the cabin walls. And then, over the hammering of his heart, Matt heard a high-pitched, tiny ... *SQUEAK!*

Squeak? Holding his breath, Matt raised his head to see. The wolf was below the window, holding on to a small something. Then it lay in the grass and gulped down its prize—a mouse!

The wolf stood up to pounce, stiff-legged, on another. Matt's breath rushed out. The wolf was hungry all right. But just for the kind of food it should eat, as Dad had said.

"Take as many of these pests as you can!" Matt called to the wolf through the window. "Dad and I can't do anything about them. But you can!"

As the wolf pounced again, Matt opened the laptop. He wrote every detail of his evening with the wolf. The story would be waiting for Dad when he returned in the morning—long after the smart, shy wolf had moved on in search of other animals to eat.

# THE Robin family
## BY ELIZABETH FRITZ

Mr. and Mrs. Robin were building a nest. For several days they had been flying to a branch halfway up our pear tree. As they flew, wisps of stuff dangled from their beaks.

From our porch we could see the nest taking shape. It was just a bit bigger around than a softball.

Mrs. Robin wove coarse grass, twigs, bits of paper, cloth, and string to make the base and sides. Next she brought mud in her bill from our flower beds where snow still lay in patches. She smeared the mud on the inside of the woven nest. Then she plopped down in the muddy nest and wiggled around and around, pressing the mud against the sides with her breast and wings. When the plastering job was dry she lined the cup-shaped nest with soft grasses and downy feathers.

The nest building took three days. Sometimes Mr. Robin perched up high on an electric pole and trilled to warn all other robins that they had better stay out of his territory. He didn't mind trespassing sparrows or thrushes, but he would puff out his red breast and peck at other robins.

One night the wind roared through the pear tree. Would the nest be blown out? The next morning it was still there, and Mrs. Robin was settled in, her tail sticking up like a flag.

Day after day Mr. Robin brought her food. Once we saw him astride the nest, guarding it while she had a little outing. If we craned our necks we could see four blue eggs.

About two weeks later we awoke to see Mr. and Mrs. Robin flying around with pieces of blue eggshell in

their beaks. The babies had broken out of their shells, and the parents were cleaning house.

We could see four big yellow beaks and the bright orange insides of four hungry mouths popping up from the nest. These babies were hungry! Mr. and Mrs. Robin pulled juicy earthworms from the ground. Between the two of them they fed the babies worms and insects at least 50 times a day.

By the end of two weeks the naked, squirmy babies had grown tan and brown feathers, and had speckled breasts. The babies were now so big they hung over the sides of the nest. When they slept their heads drooped over the edge. They pushed and shoved each other, trying to stretch their wings.

Finally one of the babies climbed out of the cramped quarters. We could barely see him on the branch close to the nest. His speckled breast blended in with the tree branches. He made a move to get back in, but the other babies cheeped a clear and noisy "No!" Number One inched his way along the branch. Before he had gone very far, Number Two stood up on the edge of the nest and stepped onto the branch. As he moved away, Numbers Three and Four followed.

By this time we had lost track of Number One. Then we saw Mrs. Robin on the ground below the tree, a grasshopper in her mouth. Number One flapped his wings and fluttered to the ground—and she gave him the grasshopper as a reward.

At that very moment a huge gray cat sprang to the top of the fence and jumped down into the yard. Shrill warning cries from Mr. and Mrs. Robin filled the air. Number One crouched low in the grass and

stayed very still. The other three hid on the tree branch.

We rushed for the garden hose, hoping to scare off the cat with a spray of water, but Mrs. Robin was quicker. She ran along the ground, a few feet ahead of the cat, fluttering one wing. Mr. Robin hovered above, beating his wings and scolding the cat with sharp cries.

The cat paused for a second to look up at Mr. Robin, then pounced at Mrs. Robin. But quick as a flash she flew up out of his reach. Her flut-

tering wing had been a trick to draw attention away from the babies. We turned on the hose full force, and the cat leaped away over the fence.

It didn't take long for the young robins to pass their flying lessons and go off on their own. Soon the freckles would disappear from their breasts and they would have orange-red ones like their parents'. They would find their own worms and insects that summer and fly south for the winter.

By now the flowers were blooming, and the days were warm. We were just saying how much we

missed our robin family when we looked up into the pear tree and saw Mrs. Robin's tail sticking up like a flag from the nest. She was nesting again. From above came Mr. Robin's cheery song. Soon we would see a second family of robins born, raised, and sent out into the world.

# THE GHOST IN ROOM 113

BY MARIE VENTURA

Yesterday was Friday the 13th. It was a day I'll never forget.

Oh, I'm Madison Rigg, and I live in Rhode Island. I was at school like any other day. The sky was dark, and it was raining, but our classroom was hot and stuffy. Our teacher, Mr. Perez, opened the door to the playground to let in some air, but it didn't help much. We were still miserable.

"That's Friday the 13th for you—very unlucky," Alejandro said.

Mr. Perez told Alejandro not to be silly. He said it's just a superstition that Friday the 13th is unlucky. Bad things will happen only if you let the idea of an unlucky day scare you. That's what he said. But weird things happened anyway.

The sounds began just after our math lesson. They came from the coatroom. They were creepy and creaking and hoarse—like some kid making noises low in his throat. Keisha thought it was Aiden, the boy in front of her. He liked to cause trouble. Keisha kicked the back of his chair. But when Aiden turned around to tell her to cut it out, the noise came again. This time, even Mr. Perez heard it.

"What's going on over there?" He asked, and frowned at Aiden as he waited for an answer.

"Keisha's kicking my chair, and I didn't do nothing!" Aiden answered.

"Didn't do *anything*, Aiden," Mr. Perez corrected, and went to the coatroom. The creepy noise came again—then again. By this time, the whole class was getting nervous.

"Bet it's a ghost!" said Jacob.

Emily looked terrified. "Oh, no!" she cried. "I want to go home! Friday the 13th is a cursed day!"

"Oh, stop it," I said. "It's no use getting scared. What we've got to do is investigate! That's the only way to find out what's really going on."

"OK, but how do you investigate a ghost?" Logan asked.

"You don't," Mr. Perez said, closing the coatroom door, "because there *are* no ghosts. And there's nothing in the coatroom either."

"Then what were those noises?" Logan asked.

Mr. Perez sighed and sat on his desk. "I want you all to listen up," he said. "You're upset because you think Friday the 13th is unlucky, right?"

We nodded.

"I'll tell you a secret," he said. "Friday the 13th is never unlucky in Rhode Island. Any bad luck that comes here gets canceled right out. Can anyone guess why?"

We couldn't.

"Think about it," he said. "Delaware is the first state, right? And Rhode Island is ..."

"The 13th state!" we all called out.

"But doesn't that *double* the bad luck?" I asked.

Mr. Perez smiled. "Nope," he said. "Because that's a *good* 13. The good 13 and the bad 13 cancel each other out. So, in Rhode Island, Friday the 13th is just a normal day. You can all relax!"

We almost believed him. I could see that Emily did. But then Keisha screamed.

"THE GHOST!!!" she shrieked, leaping up from her desk. "THE GHOST TOUCHED MY FOOT!"

Mr. Perez squeezed the bridge of his nose. "Keisha, please ..."

"No, it did. I'm telling you it did!" she cried. "I felt it, all cold and clammy and horrible!"

Alejandro frowned. "But there can't be a ghost! Not if Mr. Perez is right about the 13s canceling out each other!"

We looked at each other nervously and then looked all around the classroom. That's when Aiden noticed the number on our classroom door.

"Look!" he cried. "Our room number is 113! Wouldn't that cancel out the canceling out?"

"Hey, yeah!" said Alejandro. "That means, in this room, Friday the 13th is still on!"

Mr. Perez groaned. Emily started to sniffle.

The ghostly sounds began again, filling the room with horrible croaks.

"It's coming from over there," I said, running to the bookcase.

"It's not fair!" Emily sobbed, completely terrified. "I don't *want* to see a ghost!"

"Then you don't want to look here," I said, staring at the books in disbelief. *"Whoa!"*

The thin paperbacks on the bottom row were moving forward, a few at a time, all by themselves, as if invisible fingers were tugging at them. I thought my heart would thump right out of my chest!

"Something's back there," Mr. Perez said, and for the first time I could tell he was scared, too. Emily let out a wail. That sealed it. It was time to find this ghost, once and for all.

I crouched down and grabbed the bottom row of books, yanking them to the floor. Mr. Perez jumped. I don't think he expected me to do that. But then I stood up with a grin on my face, triumphantly clutching our "ghost" in my hands.

"What is it?" Jacob asked as everyone crowded around me. "Is it a monster?"

"Well, that all depends," I grinned. "Are you scared of frogs?"

"Frogs?" Jacob sounded disappointed. "You mean it wasn't a ghost doing all that stuff?"

"Nope," I said. "Just a frog. It must have hopped in through the open door."

"Congratulations, Madison, for cracking the case!" Mr. Perez exclaimed. "This is just the weather for frogs. You see, everybody? There's nothing scary about Friday the 13th. Only what your imaginations make of it."

*Yeah right*, I thought. But I didn't say that. Instead, I asked, "Can we keep the frog, Mr. Perez?"

But Mr. Perez had had quite enough of frogs, thank you very much. He told me to let it go outside. I did better than that. I took it to the pond at the edge of the school playground. It's still there, I bet, swimming around with its froggy feet and catching flies. But I'll tell you one thing: I don't think it'll hop into our classroom again!

# Green Velvet Princess
## BY RUTH HIGBIE

Makayla liked to hike in the woods and fields whenever she could. On rainy days she liked to read.

One stormy afternoon she found a fairy tale in an old book. It was called "The Princess Worm." A jealous, ugly witch changed a beautiful princess into a caterpillar. The witch laughed when she saw the princess crawling on the ground. She told the princess she could change back only if a prince kissed her.

"Just a fairy tale," said Makayla, looking out the window. "No way can you change into something completely different."

The next day the sun shone. As soon as she was dressed, Makayla went outdoors. As she ran down the path through the pine trees, she saw a big caterpillar. It looked as if it were made of green velvet. It had a row of white spots down its sides. Long, delicate white hairs covered its body, which was about as long as Makayla's thumb. Near its head was a circle of eight golden spikes. To Makayla they looked almost like a crown.

"It's the Princess," whispered Makayla to herself, playing make-believe. "She must have been wearing a green velvet gown with pearl buttons when the wicked witch put a spell on her. She was wearing her gold crown and a thin white cape.

"Look. Little gold knobs run all down her back, so she wore a long gold necklace too. Poor thing. She can be the princess in my terrarium."

Makayla carefully cut off part of the pine branch where the caterpillar was crawling. She put the branch and the caterpillar into the terrarium she had made from an old fish tank.

The caterpillar's three pairs of front legs were bright yellow. "The Princess was wearing gloves," said Makayla. Four pairs of short, soft, green legs held tight to the pine twig. So did a pair at the end. Those legs were black and gold. The Princess's long gown must have had beautiful black and gold trim, Makayla decided.

The yellow legs grabbed the tip of a pine needle. Slowly they worked to pull the needle into the caterpillar's mouth. The caterpillar chewed away until it had eaten the whole needle. Then the golden legs reached for another needle and brought it to the caterpillar's mouth.

Makayla never saw her princess caterpillar do anything but eat. Every day or so, when the Princess had eaten all the needles, Makayla set a fresh branch in the moist soil of the terrarium.

Makayla looked on her tablet and found a Web site with a picture of her caterpillar. The one in the picture didn't look as pretty as *her* "princess." The site said the caterpillar was the *larva* of the imperial moth.

"I knew she was special!" cried Makayla. "Imperial means she'll be an empress. That's even better than a princess or a queen. But how can a prince find her here?"

The Web site said imperial caterpillars eat pine needles and other types of tree leaves. Most of these caterpillars are green, but some are brown.

The next morning when Makayla checked the terrarium, the caterpillar was gone! She *couldn't* have gotten out! Where could she be? Then Makayla saw a wrinkled, dark green lump on the dirt under the pine branch.

"She's dead!" cried Makayla. "Now the prince will never find her!"

But the wrinkled lump began to twist and turn. It wiggled down into the soil and disappeared.

What was happening? Makayla carefully brushed away a bit of soil. Then she watched her princess caterpillar squirm and wiggle right out of its skin. All that was left of the beautiful green velvet gown was a crumpled rag. Now the princess caterpillar didn't look like a caterpillar anymore. And it didn't look like a princess, either. Instead it had changed into a creamy white "egg"—very soft and about half as long as Makayla's little finger. Gently, Makayla pushed some soil back over it.

Two days later she peeked under the soil again. Something else had happened. The soft white sac had turned hard and shiny brown.

"It's a *pupa*," said Makayla. "Next summer

it will turn into an adult moth. Most moths spin silk cocoons to protect themselves. But this one digs into the ground. That's just as safe, I guess. But it will be a long wait before something happens."

Makayla decided to put her terrarium in the shed. She knew the pupa had to stay cold before it could change into a moth.

Months passed. The pine branch turned brown. Makayla checked the pupa each day.

One morning when summer finally came she saw a strange shapeless thing on the dead branch. It had a fat body, and four wrinkly pieces hung down from its sides. As Makayla watched, a wonderful thing happened.

The wrinkles smoothed out. "Wow!" Makayla cried. "They've turned into *wings*!"

Makayla carried the tank outside. She sat down beside it and watched. The moth's body turned to yellow with purple stripes. Slowly the wings spread out and stiffened. They were nearly as wide across as Makayla's hand. As they dried, they became a lovely soft yellow with pale purple spots on them. A wavy purple band ran across the wings. This creature was even more beautiful than the green velvet caterpillar had been. "I guess it's *not* impossible for something to change completely!" she said.

By evening, the moth's wings had grown strong. Makayla watched as the imperial moth spread them and fluttered off into the dark.

"Bye-bye, Empress," she called. "The magic worked! One day soon your prince, another imperial moth, will find you. Then you will lay eggs. They will turn into green velvet princesses just like you were when I first found you."

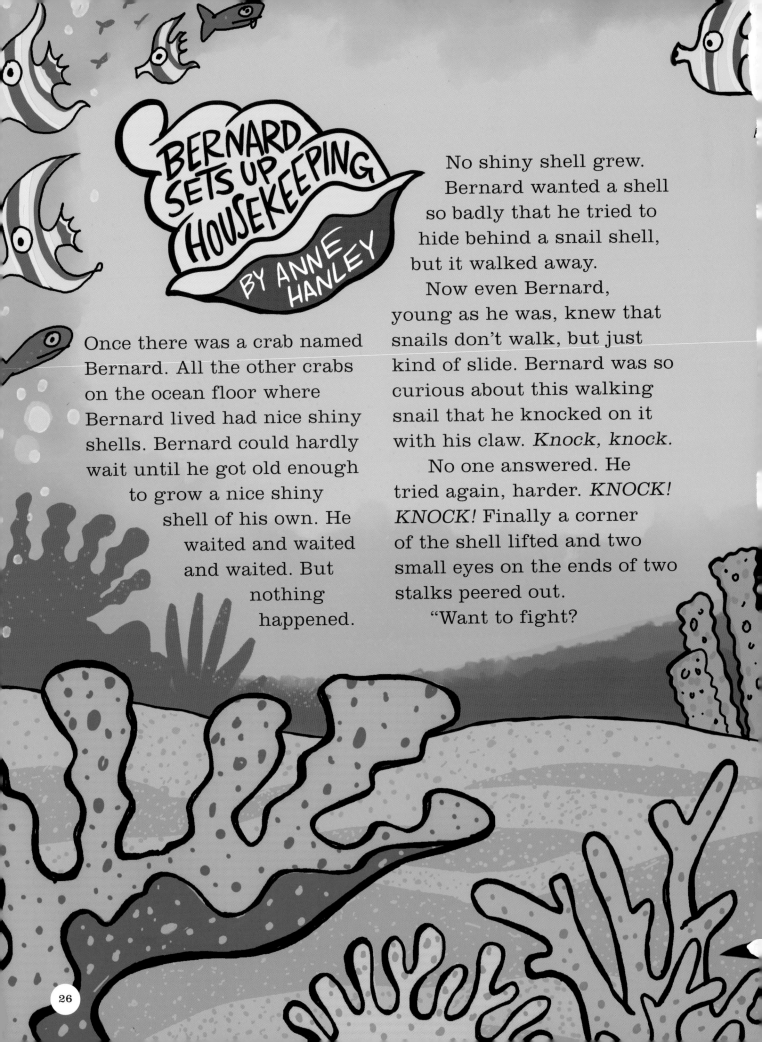

# BERNARD SETS UP HOUSEKEEPING

## BY ANNE HANLEY

Once there was a crab named Bernard. All the other crabs on the ocean floor where Bernard lived had nice shiny shells. Bernard could hardly wait until he got old enough to grow a nice shiny shell of his own. He waited and waited and waited. But nothing happened.

No shiny shell grew. Bernard wanted a shell so badly that he tried to hide behind a snail shell, but it walked away.

Now even Bernard, young as he was, knew that snails don't walk, but just kind of slide. Bernard was so curious about this walking snail that he knocked on it with his claw. *Knock, knock.*

No one answered. He tried again, harder. *KNOCK! KNOCK!* Finally a corner of the shell lifted and two small eyes on the ends of two stalks peered out.

"Want to fight?

Want to fight?" squeaked a tiny voice.

"No," said Bernard, "I just want to find out *what you are.*"

"*Who* are *you?*" asked the tiny voice.

"I'm Bernard, a crab without a shell."

The voice inside the shell began to laugh. It laughed so hard that the whole shell shook, and finally it fell over on its side.

"Come out of there this minute!" yelled Bernard, who didn't like to be laughed at.

"Promise you won't try to take my shell," said the voice.

"Of course not," Bernard said. "What would I want with your silly shell?"

The creature laughed and stuck out two orange claws.

They looked just like Bernard's claws—the right one a little bigger than the left one. Then came a head, four long legs and four short ones. And finally it pulled out its long, soft, banana-shaped tummy. The creature looked just like Bernard, only bigger.

"Hey!" said Bernard. "You're not a snail! You look just like a crab! What kind of a creature *are* you?"

"Well, we're both hermit crabs," said the creature, still laughing.

"You don't have a nice shiny shell either," said Bernard, with great satisfaction.

"Of course not. Hermit crabs don't grow their own shells. We live inside empty snail shells. And now, Bernard, if you'll excuse me, I feel terribly nervous out here."

And with that, the crab climbed back into its shell.

"Wait!" yelled Bernard. "Where can I find a shell to live in?" Bernard shook and shook the shell, but there was no answer. Then two pairs of legs came out and the shell slowly walked away.

Bernard started house hunting, but every shell he found was occupied, either by a live snail or by another hermit crab.

Finally he found an empty snail shell, but it was very small. He crawled in headfirst to look around. He was stuck! He pushed the shell with both his claws and all his feet. He pushed and pushed. Finally the tight shell popped off.

"Now how did that other crab do it?" he wondered. He stood back a minute to think. "If I go in backward, I'll come out frontward. Yes, that must be the right way to do it!"

Bernard tried backing into the tiny shell, but he still didn't fit.

Then he noticed a bigger shell nearby. He climbed out of the tiny shell and into the bigger shell—tummy first, then feet, then head. His new house fit perfectly!

He strutted up and down, stopping to admire his reflection in a scallop shell lined with shiny mother-of-pearl. Then he saw a huge shell! It had more designs and lots of pretty colors. He climbed into it, but this shell was so huge and so heavy, he could barely move.

Bernard decided to try on a few more houses. He was having a grand time—until he saw a starfish slithering up behind him. (Starfish like to eat hermit crabs.) Bernard scrambled back to the shell that fitted him perfectly. He crawled into it just in time!

Since shells don't have doors, Bernard held his big right claw in front of the entrance to close it off. He got his claw up just as the starfish was covering his shell and his claw with hundreds of tiny tube feet.

Now a starfish's feet work something like little

suction cups. They stick to things and hold tight. The starfish stuck its feet all around Bernard's shell and pulled. Bernard curled his tummy around the inside of the shell and held on tight with his small rear legs. The starfish kept pulling, but Bernard kept holding. Finally the starfish gave up.

When the pulling stopped and Bernard thought it was safe, he peeked out. *Better to have a house that fits. Why, that one shell was so big, I wouldn't have been able to hold on tight. I would have been eaten out of house and home!* he thought, laughing at his own joke.

He started walking along the ocean floor to show off his new house to the other crabs. He walked a little way and discovered a pretty flower growing on a rock.

"I think I'll decorate my house and really show off to those other crabs," he said to himself as he picked the flower.

Bernard had no sooner put the pretty orange sea flower on his roof than he heard a tiny voice. "Hi," said the tiny voice, "I'm Annie, and I'm glad to be your buddy."

Bernard pushed his head out farther and stretched his eye stalks, trying to get a peek at his roof. "I don't believe it," said Bernard, "a talking flower that thinks I'm her buddy." "I'm not a flower," said Annie. "I'm a sea anemone, and I should think you would be glad to have me for a buddy."

"And just why should I be glad to have you for a buddy?" he asked.

She waved several long, feathery tentacles near one of Bernard's eyes. "You'll find out soon enough," she said in a teasing but friendly voice.

"Well, I guess I'll let you ride along for a little while," said Bernard, who wasn't sure he was doing the right thing.

Annie settled down comfortably on Bernard's shell. Her tentacles swayed back and forth like flowers in a breeze.

"I don't think I like the idea of a talking anemone

living on my roof," mumbled Bernard after a while. "I'll get rid of her soon enough. As soon as I see a new shell, I'll ditch this one, climb into the new one and run away without her."

Bernard stopped to chew on a piece of old seaweed. As he chopped away with his claws, tiny pieces floated up toward Annie. Bernard suddenly spied Annie stuffing tiny pieces of seaweed into her mouth with her busy tentacles.

"Well," he grumbled, "not only is she a talking anemone, but she's a freeloader as well!"

A little while later, he spied an empty, plain-looking whelk shell. *It's a little less than I have now,* he thought, *but I'll take it, just to get away.*

He was just about to make a run for it when Annie yelled out, "Starfish!" Bernard retreated into his shell as far as he could. Annie began waving her tentacles furiously. Bernard stayed very still. He peeked between his claws to see the starfish creeping closer. It was huge! Bernard thought he was finished this time—he would never be able to outmuscle *this* starfish.

Just as Bernard was thinking about what a short life he had had, he saw the starfish scurrying away as fast as its five arms could carry it.

"You can come out now," whispered Annie.

"What in the world happened?" gasped Bernard.

"See these tentacles? They can sting! I can use them to scare away *all* your enemies—octopuses, squid, and starfish. How about it, can I stay?" asked Annie.

Bernard was still too nervous to talk, but he waved his claw up and down to mean, "Yes, you can stay."

When Bernard calmed down, he started to think. *If one anemone can scare away a starfish, just think how safe I'd be with a bunch of anemones on my shell!* So he crawled around gathering anemones until his shell was covered with them.

And Bernard and his mobile home and his anemone friends are probably to this very day still together on the ocean floor.

Miguel crushed a chunk of dried dirt under his high tops, sending a puff of dust into the air. It made a loud, crunching noise. He glanced nervously over his shoulder at a crowd of tough-looking, tank-topped teens. *Good—they didn't hear me,* he thought. The teens were still squatting in a half-circle, their backs toward him.

Miguel's shoulders relaxed. *Safe.* He almost smiled as he came around the pink plaster wall and dodged behind a scraggly, flowering bush.

The narrow track twisted through tall, dry weeds. As Miguel followed it, his T-shirt caught on a branch of a small tree.

Beyond still more trees, a breath of coolness and a taste of dampness hit Miguel. The air felt as good as a cold soda on a hot day. He entered a tiny patch of green and dropped to his knees right there on the thick grass.

As always, the moist, cool shade and clear pool of water gave Miguel a sense of peace and security. It was the only place where he felt safe. He bent over to look into the water.

"Hi, Jacquín," he called to a small fish. "Yo, Diego—still the biggest fish in the pond? Hey there, Tomás, you OK?" Miguel's nose almost touched the water as he checked the fish.

Suddenly Miguel heard a splash. He glanced around with wide-open eyes. Did someone throw a rock? There was no one to be seen. When he looked back at the tiny pond, he saw the outline of a sleek green frog on the bottom.

"That splash didn't scare me," he told the frog, even though it was still on the bottom. "I just don't want any strangers here," Miguel explained. "This is *my* place, you know."

Miguel's hand touched one of the big, gray rocks he'd used to dam the pond. "I built this place. The day I ran from them," he said as he glanced back in the direction of the teenagers, "I crashed into this place. Hah, you should have seen it then. Tires, trash, broken furniture—and old Diego swimming in a puddle so small that a dog could drink it dry."

The frog, Miguel's audience of one, swam up and climbed out onto a rock.

"It just didn't seem fair. A fish all closed in like that. A guy's got to have hope, you know. Got to have a chance to move out, to grow,

to be somebody special." Miguel looked at the fish swimming calmly in the water.

"So I pulled all that old trash away. *I* did it! And I built this dam to make the water a little deeper. Now look. Grass came up. The water's clear. And two little fish showed up from some- where."

Miguel sat silently. The heat and cement seemed far away. Watching the fish swim past a big hunk of rusting metal, he frowned. That car bumper had mocked him from the first day. He'd tugged and dug and kicked. But it was still stuck, a blot on the beauty of his little corner of nature.

He looked over at the car bumper—and his mouth fell open. There were dig marks around it. The grass had been trampled as if a strug- gle had occurred. Miguel's back stiffened. He looked around, searching each bush for the invader.

"Hey!" said a voice behind Miguel's back. Miguel whirled around and stood with fists up, facing the intruder.

"What are you doing in my place?" Miguel said, feeling smaller than ever as he faced the invader. It was a light-skinned boy with straight, blond hair and long, thin arms and legs.

The blond boy backed up a step at the anger in Miguel's black eyes. "Hey, chill out. I'm not after any trouble."

"Then why are you here?"

The blond boy shrugged his thin shoulders. "You wouldn't understand."

"Try me."

"I live in the development." He pointed to a group of buildings in the opposite direction from Miguel's small home. "It's wall-to-wall people and no place to breathe. When it gets hot like this, the place is nasty. I just got to get away. So the other day, I found this place …" He looked around as his voice trailed off.

"Go on," Miguel said.

"Who are you to tell me what to do?" The boy moved two steps closer, and Miguel saw that he was carrying a stick. Miguel stepped back without thinking.

"Watch out!"

the blond boy cried. "Don't step on Sam!"

Miguel glanced down and saw the small frog hopping away from his foot. "You call him *Sam?*"

"Now, listen," the blond boy said as his face turned red with embarrassment.

"Anybody can see he should be called Pablo!" Miguel told him.

The boy froze, and then grinned. "You're kidding. Pablo? No way. *George,* maybe."

Miguel and the boy turned and bent toward the frog for a closer view. But the frog just jumped into the water and disappeared.

"He should be called *Adios,*" Miguel said with a laugh.

"He'll come back if you're quiet for a while," the other boy said.

Miguel studied the boy standing next to him. "You come here often?"

"Just started," the boy said. "Today, I swore I'd get rid of that old bumper."

"I've tried too. It doesn't want to come loose." Miguel kicked at his old enemy, but the metal didn't budge. His eyes met the blue eyes of the other boy for a long moment. "Maybe, together, we could get it out?"

"Yeah—let's try!" A grin split the blond boy's face as he stuck out a hand. "My name's Alex."

Miguel gripped his hand and smiled. "I'm Miguel. Come on, we've got work to do. Let's get this trash out of …" He paused a minute. "Out of *Sam's* home."

# DIRTY FACE LEARNS TO FISH
## By Richard C. Davids

The world seemed wonderful to Dirty Face, a little brown bear who lived with her big, furry mother beside the McNeil River in Alaska. She got her name from her muzzle, which was always black, no matter how carefully and how often her mother licked it.

Dirty Face didn't care. She was happy. There were plenty of roots and berries and mice to eat. The river was clear and full of salmon, and Mother Bear was a fine fisher. She could grab fish in her big mouth and dig up ground squirrels with her curved claws, which were half as long as a pencil. All Dirty Face had to do was watch and feast.

When Dirty Face was three years old, Mother Bear had twin male cubs. After that, life was never the same for Dirty Face. Every time she came near her little brothers—who looked like roly-poly Teddy bears—Mother Bear snarled and growled. And one day Mother Bear and her twin babies walked away, leaving Dirty Face all alone.

Dirty Face was very sad. Before long she grew very hungry. She dug for roots in the sand bars but couldn't find any. She climbed the riverbank and sniffed for ground squirrels.

But her mother had already found them.

Sadly, Dirty Face returned to the river and gazed out over the cold, cascading water. If you were a little bear, how would you catch fish with only your mouth and two bare paws? Dirty Face inched her way out on a shallow reef. She saw the salmon darting past on their way upstream to lay their eggs. Dirty Face should have watched more closely when her mother had fished!

A salmon paused. Dirty Face batted at it with her left paw so hard she slipped and fell into the swirling water. She crawled out and shook herself.

In all the world there was no colder, sadder bear than Dirty Face.

But hunger made her try again. Though she was still a cub, she weighed 300 pounds. By the time she would be eight and a grownup, she would be three times that big. So you see

why Dirty Face had to eat. Besides, she could eat only in summer, because all winter she would doze in a den hidden beneath the deep snow.

She waded out in the water and stood on her hind legs. She could see the fish better that way. A herring gull came to watch. Dirty Face stood and waited until the cold water made her feet ache. Once again she went to shore and shivered.

She bellowed for her mother but there was no answer. All day she had been without food. Once when she wasn't looking, a salmon leaped out of the water beside her. The smell of fish made her even hungrier. She jumped into the river, lost her footing on the rocks and was covered with white spray.

Struggling to find her footing, she felt a stick. But it wasn't a stick. It moved. Her claws sank deep and held it—a fat, wriggling salmon!

She grabbed it in her mouth and splashed her way to shore, paused and shook herself so hard the droplets made a shiny mist around her. The gull screamed above her. This was fun! Getting your own fish was even better than having your mother catch fish for you. Being a grownup was going to be exciting.

Dirty Face learned that salmon sometimes rest before leaping upstream over the rocks, and in the foaming water they couldn't see her. She learned to feel for them and when to pounce. Sometimes with one fish already in her mouth, she would try to catch another. Often she would disappear completely under water. Now and then she would dive and go head over heels. She was in the water a third of the day, but all the exercise kept her warm.

By August, Dirty Face was the best fisher on the whole river!

# Meadow Mystery

By Beverly Letchworth

Come into my meadow. Pretty, isn't it? See the Queen Anne's lace, the red and white clover, the timothy hay? The yellow hawkweed is blooming too.

What, you don't know who I am? Or where I am? You're not supposed to. If you could find me right off, it would mean I'm not very well hidden.

There is danger in my meadow, you know. Big creatures eat many little ones. I can't be too careful. See the wasps buzzing around? They are really my enemies.

I could tell you who I am, but wouldn't you like to guess first? No, I'm not the toad sitting under the strawberry plant. And I'm not the white-footed mouse hiding in the grass. I've already given you some clues.

I am small—much smaller than a toad or a mouse. All around the meadow there are thousands of my kind. I'm not full-grown yet. When I am grown up, I'll be one of the best hoppers around. I'll be able to land on your hand when you walk through the meadow, then leap off so quickly you'll never find me again.

A grasshopper? Wrong! I knew you'd think that! But don't get in a snit. You're on the right track. I am an insect, but not a grasshopper.

You say you still can't see me? Well, I'm hiding. Look closely at the red clover plants around you. What do you see?

Well, I have to give you more credit. You're right. You see a little blob of white foam. That's my shelter. I built it. Isn't it grand? I hide in here. It protects me from the sun and keeps me nice and moist, too.

Do you see me inside? Of course not! Take a plant stem and try to find me. Yes, the bubbly stuff is sticky. It helps my shelter hold its shape. You see, I stay on plants and suck the juices from them. Most of this sap passes right through me and comes out my tail end as a special liquid called honeydew. Then I blow air into the honeydew until it becomes a bubbly foam.

I can feel you poking around, but you haven't found me yet. Isn't my foam great protection? If you were a wasp flying over me right now, you wouldn't be able to see me through the thick foam. Even if a wasp did strike, chances are it would miss, because I would have skittered to another part of my shelter.

Okay, I'll stop moving now so you can find me. Careful, now. Let me crawl out on the stem.

I guess I'm not much to look at—just a yellow insect only as long as a grain of rice. Didn't my bubbly home give you a clue? I'm a *spittlebug!* Some people call me a *froghopper.*

Right now I'm still growing. I am a *nymph.* As an adult I'll be bigger and have wings. Then I'll leave my foam shelter to hop around the meadow. Maybe I'll hop on you!

In the fall we spittlebugs lay eggs that won't hatch until spring, when a new crop of spittlebug nymphs arrives. Next summer there will be more bubbly homes all around the meadow.

Please put me back now. I feel very uneasy out in the open. In just a minute I'll be buried deep in my foam again. Do you see some of the other homes of my neighbors? Look on the clover plants. Yes, there are lots of us spittlebugs here in the meadow.

Well, it's been nice meeting you. You've been very gentle and kind with me. And you were patient with my little game of *guess who*.

If you'll excuse me now, I would like to finish my dinner. Come back in a few weeks when I and the other spittlebugs are grown. With a little luck and a sharp eye, you may get to know many of us.

# THE ALLEY BEHIND OUR HOUSE ~ NATHAN ZIMELMAN

An alley ran along the back of our house. Flowers that weren't found anywhere else in town grew here. The grass was high and always swayed, even with only the tiniest of breezes.

Pink noses twitched. Gray forms hurried. Grasshoppers hopped. Bees bumbled. Butterflies inspected the flowers. Kids prowled about seeking adventures. The alley was a place where adventures could be found. Even Herman, our family cat—whom we tried to keep inside—kept sneaking out into the alley for adventures of his own.

It was a fine place ...

"It is a horrible place!" That's what Ms. Millicent Chillington said. We kids called her "Ms. Nosey," but not so she could hear us. She went from house to house, thrusting out a paper. "Sign on the

48

line and we will make the City Council cover this alley with asphalt, the way a proper alley should be," she said.

Most people were afraid to disagree with Millicent Chillington, so lots of neighbors signed her paper. She didn't ask us kids to sign. We didn't count, I guess.

"We kids like the alley the way it is," I complained to my father.

"Not to worry," he said.

"The City Council won't do anything. They never do."

But he was wrong. The first day of summer vacation, big men turned up with trucks and diggers. They scraped the alley down to hard-packed dirt where it seemed like nothing could possibly grow. Then trucks drove in, loaded with gravel and asphalt. When the last machine left, the alley was shiny and black—and empty.

Nobody walked down the alley. Nobody drove down it. Unless somebody wanted to go no place in a hurry, there was no reason to. There was nothing to see there.

Fall came, and I started middle school. Many winters and springs and summers and falls went by. My friends and I went to high school and college and then moved away from the neighborhood.

The cold winters caused the asphalt to crack. Then springs came, full of showers and sunshine. Seeds floated in, wedging into the cracks. Buds peered out. After a few more years, it became hard to see the asphalt of the alley through all the blossoms.

Grass waved in the breeze. Pink noses twitched. Gray forms hurried. Grasshoppers hopped. Bees bumbled. Butterflies inspected the flowers.

Visiting my parents one beautiful summer day, I opened the back door. Their new kitten scooted out before I could stop him. "Meow," he called, which said it all, as he entered the magic of the alley that ran along the back of our house.

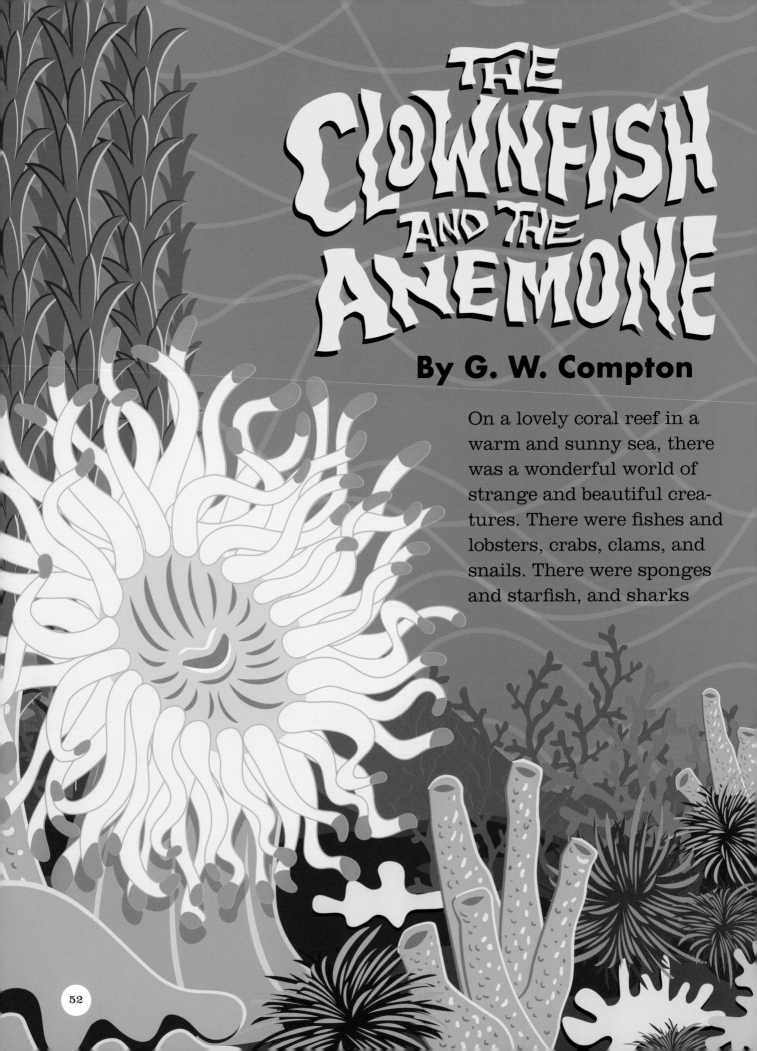

# THE CLOWNFISH AND THE ANEMONE

## By G. W. Compton

On a lovely coral reef in a warm and sunny sea, there was a wonderful world of strange and beautiful creatures. There were fishes and lobsters, crabs, clams, and snails. There were sponges and starfish, and sharks with big tails. Seahorses, jellyfish, shrimps, and morays. Scallops and turtles, sea fans, and rays.

That's not all.

The jumble of coral that made up the reef was home to hundreds and hundreds of different sea creatures of all shapes and sizes. There were fast swimmers, slow swimmers, creatures that crept, creatures that crawled, and some that just sat still, scarcely moving at all—like one very pretty sea anemone.

It looked like a garden flower with long white petals with pink tips. But the Anemone wasn't a flower; it was an animal. The white petals with pink tips were really tentacles. They were the Anemone's arms. In the middle of all the tentacles was the Anemone's small pink mouth.

The Anemone couldn't swim—anemones can't. And it couldn't see. Anemones have no eyes. Mostly it just sat holding onto a coral. Once in a while it would slide on its bottom to another place on the coral, but very slowly—slower than a snail.

The Anemone just sat and waited until some food came along and touched its tentacles.

Gotcha!

It used the tentacles like

fingers to push the food into its small pink mouth. Each tentacle had thousands and thousands of tiny stinging cells on it. If anything touched a sting cell, it would shoot out a very small dart. Each dart was sharp as a needle and had poison in it. The poison could kill very small fishes or paralyze them so they couldn't get away.

The poison hurt big fishes and made them steer clear.

All fishes kept away from the Anemone's tentacles. All except for one small fish on the reef: a clownfish.

Like all other clownfishes, she was about as big as your little finger. She could swim and she could see. She had no problem catching enough to eat. The Clownfish was one of the prettiest fishes on the reef. Like many other clownfishes, she had a plump little body, black as the night, with two white stripes—one near her head, one near her tail. Her face was purest gold, with big bright eyes and a mouth shaped like a kiss. The small fat body made the Clownfish look like something good to eat, especially to big, hungry fishes.

The Clownfish was very small. A big hungry fish could easily gobble her up. Now, how could the Clownfish keep from being eaten? Turns out there is a way.

The Clownfish began a friendship with the Anemone. She swam a "getting-to-know-you" dance around the Anemone. Up and down and way around, she went. Up and down and way around, closer and closer. The little

Clownfish curved to brush gently against the Anemone's stinging tentacles—time and again, time and again. It was a lovely dance.

At first the Anemone stung the Clownfish. But she kept on brushing gently against the tentacles for almost an hour. The Anemone came to know the Clownfish. Finally the tentacles stopped stinging, and the Anemone made the Clownfish welcome. The small black fish with white stripes and a golden face nestled safely among the Anemone's tentacles. The two were partners for the rest of their lives. The other anemones and clownfishes on the reef found partners the same way.

One day a great big fish came looking for a meal. It saw the little Clownfish. With mouth wide open, the big fish darted toward the Clownfish. The Clownfish swam straight to the Anemone and hid among the tentacles. The Anemone stung the big fish very hard, and drove it away. Hiding from big hungry fish wasn't such a problem now for the Clownfish.

And the Clownfish helped the Anemone get extra food to eat. Sometimes she found bits of drifting food and took them back to the Anemone: one piece for the Anemone, one piece for the Clownfish. One for you. One for me. It was a fine partnership.

One day, instead of food, the Clownfish brought home a surprise: another clownfish—a male. The little female had found a mate. She was ready to raise a family. After getting to know each other, the Anemone welcomed the male clownfish. Both clownfishes were safe from their enemies, and their eggs would be too.

That is how three small sea creatures on a coral reef in a warm and sunny sea, made life easier—just by helping each other.

# OODLES OF BOODLES

## BY JUDY BRAUS

Once upon a time there was a village named Here. Most of the people in the village were farmers. They liked working the land, and they managed to grow enough food for everyone.

One farmer in the village wasn't happy with his farm. His name was Jag. Jag wanted to plant new kinds of vegetables and fruits. He was tired of eating the same old things. He was tired of seeing the same old animals. He was even tired of his pet dog, Rugger.

One day a stranger came to the village. The stranger was very old and had been walking a long time. He talked about a town that was far away. It was called There. He told Jag about all the strange animals and plants of There. He said the people of There had a favorite flower called a boodle. Boodles were bright red and grew on beautiful vines.

Then he described the colorful insects. He said there were huge flying ones bigger than butterflies—with spots on each wing. He also told about the field chippets, small mammals that lived in tall grasses. Chippets had blue fur and long legs and ears.

"How do I get to There?" asked Jag excitedly. "I'd really like to have boodles and chippets on my farm!"

"Well," the stranger said slowly, "I don't know if their animals and plants would fit in around Here. You see, the town of There is way over on the other side of the mountain. And things in There are a lot different from things in Here."

"Oh, I know they'll fit in, stranger,"

said Jag. "Please tell me how to get to There!"

The old man pointed toward the mountain. "Take that road until it ends. Then follow the path along the stream until it reaches the village. Remember, it's a long, long way, young fellow."

The very next day, Jag set out for There. He took bags and boxes so that he could bring back all kinds of new things from the village. He took plenty of food and a nice warm blanket.

After four days of travel,

Jag finally reached There. Just as the old man had said, there were all kinds of wonderful things he'd never seen before. Different crops grew in the fields. Strange birds flew in the sky. And the insects and flowers were unlike anything he knew.

Jag knocked on the first farmer's door. He noticed the house was made of stone, not wood like his. A woman came to the door.

"Hello, ma'am. My name is Jag and I'm from the village of Here. I've come to take some of your wonderful plants and animals back to my village."

"Come in," said the woman. "My name is Mera, and this is my farm. We're always happy to have visitors in our village. You're welcome to look around and take whatever you'd like."

That afternoon Mera showed Jag around. As they crossed a field, Jag noticed some large insects with colorful spots on their wings. They were just as the old man had described.

"What are those, Mera?" he asked, pointing.

"They are motflies," she answered.

Just as she said that, a large orange bird swooped down from a branch and snatched a motfly right out of the air.

"And that bird is called a gallow," said Mera. "They're always diving around the fields catching motflies."

"Look over there," said Jag. "What are those beasts?"

He pointed to two large animals standing in the field. Each one had a pair of long tusks sticking out of its upper jaw. And their legs were striped with bands of gold and brown.

"Those are rondles. They eat chippets and other small mammals."

"They sure are funny-looking!" Jag exclaimed. "But they're much too big for me to carry back to Here."

By the end of the afternoon Mera had given Jag several boodle plants to take home. She also put two chippets, four motflies, and two pet pips into one of his boxes. Pips were furry creatures with long, slender, spotted tails. Everyone in There had at least two pips.

"Oh, I can't wait until I get home!" cried Jag. "All my neighbors will be jealous. I'll be the only one with boodle vines growing on my fence! And you know, I probably could sell boodles and pips and make lots of money."

Mera smiled and waved as Jag started his long journey home.

The first thing Jag did when he returned was plant the boodles along his fence. Their bright red flowers would make the yard look very pretty.

Then he let the chippets and motflies loose in the field. He was sure they would be happy there.

But Jag noticed that his two pet pips weren't moving around very much. Jag was worried. He'd forgotten to ask Mera what they ate. "Oh, well," he said, "I'll feed them fruit—they're sure to like that. The pips are probably just tired after the long journey."

The next day Jag went out to work in his fields. He noticed that one row of his cornfield has been eaten up. *Probably the neighbor's goat again,* he thought.

As the days passed, things got worse for Jag. The boodle vines were growing everywhere. They wrapped around trees and shrubs and blocked out the sunlight. Without light, the trees and shrubs shriveled and died.

Then Jag noticed that there were a lot more chippets than the two he'd brought from There. He counted more than fifteen. "I guess they have a lot of babies!" he said. He couldn't believe how fast the chippets had spread. Then he remembered there were no rondles around to keep their numbers under control. He also noticed that more and more of his corn was being eaten. One day Jag watched one

of the spotted motflies land on his apple tree. Then he saw it stick its long beak into one of the fruits. It looked as if the insect were sucking out the juice. After a few minutes on one apple, it flew to another.

"Well," said Jag, with a troubled look, "at least there are only a few of them."

Most of the other animals seemed to be doing well in Here, except for the pips. They just lay around and ate hardly anything. The village healer said they were sick, but never having seen a pip before, she didn't know how to make them better.

Jag wasn't the only one having problems. His neighbor, Mrs. Piper, was upset because some kind of flying insect was ruining all her apples. And strange, furry creatures were eating Mr. Murphy's corn.

That same day, Jag noticed a small yellow beetle chewing the shingles of his roof. Then he saw another. When he climbed up for a closer look, Jag realized that there were hundreds of the beetles gnawing away at the wooden planks. He'd never seen anything like them before.

"But how did they get here from There?" he wondered. "I didn't bring any with me. Maybe they were hiding among the boodle plants I brought. No wonder the people in There have houses made of stone!"

The village council decided they had to do something. They knew Jag and his new animals and plants had caused the whole mess. They called Jag before them and said, "We have to get rid of all those weird plants and animals you brought to Here. They just don't fit in."

Jag knew the council was right. He wished he had never brought anything back.

Jag and everyone else in the village began to dig up all the boodle plants they could find. But by now the plants seemed to be everywhere! Day after day they trapped the chippets. But the animals seemed to multiply faster than the people could catch them. The villagers also caught toads in the woods and let them go in their yards and houses. They hoped the toads would eat all those pesky yellow beetles and motflies.

The two pips died and were buried before they spread any new diseases.

Then after a few weeks the villagers' luck began to change. The motflies began to die off as soon as all the apples were gone. Foxes discovered the chippets and began to keep their numbers under control. The villagers made a special shellac that they painted on their houses. It kept away all the yellow beetles. And they managed to dig up every boodle plant.

Jag knew he had been very foolish. But he and the villagers had learned a lesson the hard way. Here was a lot different from There. Animals and plants that belonged in There did *not* belong in Here. And that's the way things would stay.

OLD WITCH

By Ruth Kelley

When we moved away from Los Angeles and out to a ranch, I thought it would be the worst. No one to play with. A three-mile walk home from the school bus stop. Even going to the store was an hour-long trip in the car.

I soon discovered, though, that in the country things that seem terrible often have a good side. Because I was so lonely—and to give me something to do—my parents got me a burro. I named her Juanita.

Burros can be stubborn. But by spring, I could ride Juanita all over the canyon— at least wherever she wanted to go. That's how I discovered the "hidden valley" in the hills behind our house.

The valley is like a huge bowl that catches water from the surrounding hills. Except for the spiky yucca plants growing there, the rocky slopes of the valley were almost bare. But the bushes on the valley floor were thick, and the oak trees were huge and shady.

One day when we were up there, Juanita spooked as if she'd seen a snake. I saw nothing but a narrow trail. Since I couldn't get her to budge, I got off and followed the trail myself. It led to a big hole in the hillside. Inside were two baby foxes! When they saw me, they scurried farther into their den.

After that, every time I went back to the valley I left Juanita at home. Then I hid in the bushes to watch the den. I saw the babies a few more times, but never the parents.

Dad said foxes hunt mostly at night. So one morning before sunup, I hiked to the valley to watch the trail again. Just before daybreak, I saw a bushy gray fox. He had a ragged notch in his ear. I decided to call him "Old Notch."

That first winter and spring in our canyon, we had only seven inches of rain. By May, Juanita's pasture was almost bare. Only sticker-weeds and mustard plants grew there, which even the rabbits wouldn't eat. By summertime, even in my hidden valley, bushes were dusty, dry, and crackly. The water level in our well was so low, we had to take "miniature" showers (minute you're in, minute you're out).

Then one day in August, things got scary.

I was reading in my bedroom. Suddenly I heard the loud thrumping of a helicopter and a blaring siren—right over my head! I rushed to my window. Flames and smoke were billowing up from the ridge along the side of our dirt road.

"Get some shoes on and get ready to help!" Mom yelled. She raced around the house shutting windows and closing drapes.

Mom tried to call Dad at work. The phone was dead! The wind was blowing toward us, and the flames were traveling fast. I could smell smoke from inside the house.

By the time I'd tied my shoes, another helicopter had come. It was huge. It landed right in Juanita's pasture. Dirt and sand from the bare ground blew everywhere. Eight people in weird-looking yellow suits and hats climbed out. They carried tools that looked like a combination hoe-and-shovel. One of them waved. We couldn't see the face inside the helmet. Mom said it was probably her cousin Jessica who works on the fire crews every season. They all hurried toward the fire, and the helicopter took off again.

Mom said, "Shut Juanita in the barn. She needs to stay out of the way, and we may need to grab her quickly to get her out of here. And bring those burlap sacks and buckets by the barn door. Quick!" She sounded worried. I sure wished Dad were home. What if sparks flew over and our house caught fire?

I took care of Juanita and grabbed the buckets and burlap sacks. Choking from the smoke, I raced to where Mom was stretching out the hoses. I could hear more helicopters. I figured they were dropping water on the fire to try to keep it away from our buildings. But it was so smoky, I couldn't see them. Even if he heard about the fire, how could Dad get home through that smoke?

We put the burlap sacks

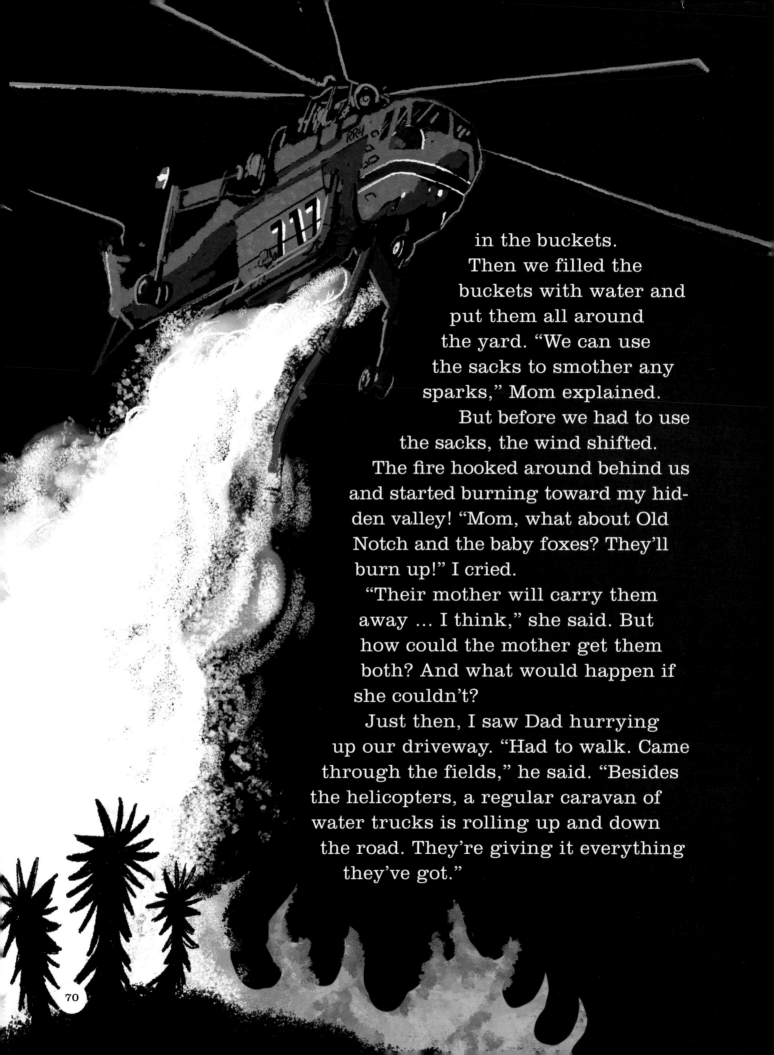

in the buckets.
Then we filled the
buckets with water and
put them all around
the yard. "We can use
the sacks to smother any
sparks," Mom explained.

But before we had to use
the sacks, the wind shifted.
The fire hooked around behind us
and started burning toward my hidden valley! "Mom, what about Old
Notch and the baby foxes? They'll
burn up!" I cried.

"Their mother will carry them
away ... I think," she said. But
how could the mother get them
both? And what would happen if
she couldn't?

Just then, I saw Dad hurrying
up our driveway. "Had to walk. Came
through the fields," he said. "Besides
the helicopters, a regular caravan of
water trucks is rolling up and down
the road. They're giving it everything
they've got."

"Why don't the helicopters drop water up there in the valley?" I asked, pointing.

"The fire up there isn't threatening any homes," Dad said. "Some of this brush *needs* to be burned out. In this climate, dead brush doesn't easily rot. It has to be burned so there can be new growth. When the rains come this winter, the ashes will act as a fertilizer for the soil."

"But what about the foxes that live there?" I wondered aloud.

"I saw a fox down in the field," Dad told me.

"Did it have a notched ear?" I asked.

"I couldn't tell."

As we watched, the smoke coming up from the valley thinned. The winds had let up, but it was too late to help the foxes. Everything in their valley was already burned.

By nighttime, the fire was almost out. In the dark, lights from the firefighters' flashlights flickered like fireflies up in the hills.

Later my dad and mom said that the fire was actually a lucky thing. The place where it had burned along the hills made a firebreak— an area where fire wouldn't easily cross. It would be a long time before enough burnable stuff would build up there. So it would be years before a big fire could come at us from that direction.

I almost cried, though, when I hiked up a few days after the fire to look at my valley. The bushes were black sticks in an ocean of gray ash. The trunks of the oaks were blackened, and most of the leaves were gone. And there was no sign of the foxes. I was so sad about it, I didn't go back all that fall or winter.

The following spring, I got a pup for my birthday. I named him Buster. He was so full of energy, I took him for a hike up to the hidden valley.

What a surprise! Clusters of baby yuccas poked out all around the dead, burned ones. The valley floor was a meadow of green grass and yellow wildflowers. The bushes that had looked like dead sticks now had tender new shoots sprouting at the bottom. All but one of the oaks had new leaves.

Buster raced toward the one dead tree, his tail wagging wildly. When I caught up with him, I discovered that the fire had burned out the whole inside of the tree. And inside, yipping at Buster were four fox kits!

I grabbed Buster. Carrying him, I hiked over to the den Old Notch had used on the other side of the valley. There were four more kits in that den—really little ones. They pointed their faces in my direction. But I'm not sure that they could see that far yet. I was so excited! If the same den was being used, at least the

parents must still be alive. So Old Notch probably made it!

I counted the fox mothers and fathers. There were at least a dozen foxes in my valley! Dad had been right. Ashes from the fire had fertilized the soil. All the new grass and bushes and acorns meant there would be plenty of food for lots of mice and rabbits and ground squirrels. And *that* meant there would be plenty of food for all the new foxes. The fire was just what my hidden valley—and the foxes—had needed.

# SNOWY TAKES A TUMBLE

BY JOSEPH J. BRANNEY

Snowy's mother landed carefully on a nest of reeds and sticks. She bent over and coughed up some fish she had caught in the marsh for her chicks. Snowy and the two other chicks tore eagerly at the food. Soon it was gone.

Snowy's mother and father took turns feeding and watching over the chicks. Sometimes the young birds ate frogs or snakes besides the small fish their parents caught for them.

Snowy and his family were *snowy egrets.* Snowy's parents had long thin legs that were good for wading in the shallow water of the marsh. Their yellow feet looked like golden slippers.

Here in the *nesting colony* or *rookery (ROOK-uh-ree),* other snowy egrets, herons, and ibises lived near Snowy's family. Like the snowy egrets, the other marsh birds made their nests of reeds and rushes. The nests rested on bent-over reeds in the marsh.

When it got too hot in the marsh, Snowy and the other egret chicks crawled to the edge of the nest to find some shade. Often one of Snowy's parents would stand on the nest to shade the chicks with its wings.

One afternoon there was a strange sound in the marsh: *Putt, putt, putt, putt, putt.* What was that? A flock of marsh birds took off from their nests, flapping their wings. Frightened by the noise and commotion, Snowy fell right over the edge of the nest. *Splash!* The people passing by in the motorboat probably didn't know that the noise would scare so many birds.

Dripping wet, Snowy crawled out of the shallow water onto some reeds. He looked up at the nest. It was only two feet above him. But it looked very far away. He squawked as loudly

as he could. His father looked down and called back to him.

Snowy tried to climb up the reeds to the nest but he couldn't. At that point it was all he could do just to stay out of the water. He was lucky that no hawks or crows knew he was there. They like to eat egret chicks.

Snowy's mother came back to the nest with more food for the egret chicks. Snowy could hear the two other chicks in the nest. They were squawking as they gobbled up the fish. He called out loudly, but his parents seemed to have forgotten him. That night Snowy missed his dinner.

He was *very* hungry.

All through the night Snowy crouched in the reeds. A large snapping turtle swam close but went on its way. Luckily no raccoons came near enough to find out they could have a chick for dinner.

Shortly before dawn Snowy's mother flew off to fish for breakfast. Snowy was so hungry that he was beginning to feel weak. He heard his mother's call overhead as she flew back to the nest.

Instead of landing on the nest, Snowy's mother landed in the reeds next to Snowy. She lowered her head and coughed up three fish for him. The hungry chick gulped down all three. Then his mother stepped toward the nest. The reeds bent underneath her as she walked. Snowy's father and the other two chicks greeted her as she stepped back onto the nest. Snowy was very lucky that his mother had brought him some food. Most egret parents won't feed a chick that has fallen out of the nest. The chick usually doesn't last very long before it starves or is eaten by a hungry animal.

Snowy now had eaten, but he was not yet out of danger. Though the nest was still above his head, the reeds his mother had bent gave him a chance. He tried to climb about on the reeds, using his bill as well as his toes to keep his balance. It was hard work. Step by step, he made his way up the reeds. Although he wobbled as he climbed, he didn't fall. Finally he made it back to the nest.

Soon Snowy and the other two egret chicks would all be strong enough to climb in and out of the nest with ease. Snowy's tumbling days were done!

# The Secret of Silver Pond

by Laura Wrang

Brandon felt excited as he biked toward the pond. There it lay, cool and still—a silver eye that winked at him in the sun. He hadn't been able to solve its secret last summer. This summer he had a feeling he would.

He pedaled to the edge of the pond and then frowned.

He hadn't expected company. Sitting on the grass was a red-haired boy.

"I've been watching you," said the boy. He raised a pair of binoculars. "See?"

Brandon didn't answer. He parked his bike and untied a shovel from the back of it.

"Treasure hunter," scoffed the boy. "You think you'll find the emerald necklace with that thing?"

"What makes you think I'm looking for it?" Brandon asked.

"Kids from the summer cabins always are. But everyone who lives here knows better. The thief threw the necklace in the water. You need a snorkel, not a shovel."

Brandon shrugged. He had heard that version of the story before. The man who stole the necklace from old Mrs. Gomez ten years ago was captured near Silver Pond. Some said he had pitched the necklace in the water before the police caught him. But others believed he had buried it. Then he died in prison without telling anyone his secret.

"I say Old Scratch threw it in," the boy said.

Brandon perked up. "Why was he called Old Scratch?"

"He used to steal small things. When folks questioned him, he just scratched his head and smiled. When the police asked him about the emerald necklace, he scratched himself all over and laughed out loud."

The boy scratched like a monkey. He looked so funny that Brandon had to smile.

"My name's Tyler," said the boy. "Can I help you dig?"

"I thought you said the necklace wasn't buried," said Brandon.

Tyler grinned. "Maybe I'm wrong."

They worked all day. First they poked sticks here and there at the muddy edge of the pond. Finding nothing there, they moved to the woods. Tyler was a big help. He knew the good places to look.

"Trees can have hollows in their trunks or holes under their roots," he said. He also knew where not to look: "That trash pit is just a few years old, so the necklace wouldn't be hidden there. And that green patch is poison ivy. We'd better stay clear."

At day's end, though empty-handed, Brandon was still set on finding the emerald necklace. To his surprise, so was Tyler.

Over the next two weeks, they combed the area together. They climbed trees to look for likely spots, searched among the plants, turned over stones, and poked in the ground.

They refilled each hole they made, so as not to spoil the area for others. In between digging, they had fun in the pond. Tyler was an ace at inventing swimming games, and he kept Brandon laughing with his jokes.

But on the fifteenth day, Brandon felt sad. "Maybe we should give up the hunt. We've looked almost everywhere."

Tyler frowned. "I've been thinking," he said slowly. "Remember that pile of stones?"

"Sure. You said that they were cracked from the heat of old campfires."

"That rock you're sitting on is cracked too," Tyler told him. "Someone could have moved it here to mark a spot."

Brandon jumped up. "It could have been Old Scratch!"

With growing excitement, Brandon rolled away the rock. Tyler seized the shovel and dug at the spot. They both gasped as he struck something hard. But when Brandon pulled it from the soil, it was just a rusty can.

The boys groaned and dropped to the ground. Brandon buried his head in his hands. That rock was his last hope. Tomorrow he was going back home. He'd never find the necklace now.

Then he raised his head and looked at Tyler. He smiled in spite of himself. He hadn't found the necklace, but he had found a new friend. Tyler and he could Skype and tweet to each other, and they could see each other again next summer.

"We'd better call it a day," said Tyler. "Want to come home with me? Mom is baking a cherry pie from scratch, and

I can't wait to have a piece."

Something clicked in Brandon's brain. "What did you say?" he asked.

"I said, 'Mom is baking a ...'"

But Brandon wasn't listening. His mind was spinning with a strange idea. He scrambled to his feet and raced toward a patch of leafy plants.

Tyler recognized the patch from when he'd seen it a couple weeks ago. "Are you crazy?" he shouted.

"No, Tyler—come on!"

Looking down through the leaves, Brandon spied a stone. He moved it aside, and when Tyler arrived with the shovel Brandon started digging. After the third shovelful, a metal box appeared. Both boys dug it out by hand and opened the lid.

Green emeralds flashed in the light like a cat's eyes. They lay in a thick chain of gold.

"We found it!" yelled Tyler. He shook his head in amazement. "I can't wait to tell the police that we solved the mystery! And won't Mrs. Gomez be surprised. I wonder if she'll give us a reward. How did you figure it out, Brandon?"

Brandon was laughing so hard that he could barely find the words. "You said your mom was baking a pie from scratch. That reminded me of Old Scratch. He used to scratch his head, but when the police asked him about the necklace, he scratched all over." He pointed down at the poison ivy where they had been digging and laughed. "We'd better get washed up, or by this time tomorrow we'll be scratching too!"

Hailey called to a man as he hurried up the steps outside the courthouse. "Hey mister, we need your help to ..." She watched as the man walked right past her and her friend Hannah. "He never even slowed down," she complained. "He just muttered, 'Snakes, yuck!'"

Even for August in South Dakota, the sun was hot. It was only ten in the morning, and both Hailey and Hannah were already wilting under their protest sign. But they stayed anyway because right now nothing was more important to them than trying to save "Snake Town."

That was their name for a rocky place along the river near their town. In the winter, hundreds and *hundreds* of plains garter snakes denned there. The girls knew that a local farmer was planning to sell the land around Snake Town to a developer who would turn it into a trailer park. So they were protesting, trying to save this special place from being destroyed. That's why they were in front of the courthouse in this brutal heat.

Now Hannah, noticing Hailey frowning, took out her earbuds. "What's the matter?" Hannah asked her friend.

"I'm not sure this protest sign really cuts it," Hailey answered.

"Yeah, 'Save Our Snakes' doesn't exactly bring a flood of tears. It doesn't even seem to make them curious," Hannah agreed. "Are you sure we're going to be on the news? I haven't seen anything yet."

"The guy who recorded our interview said it would be on the news today. Honest," Hailey replied.

"Maybe we should've made more copies of the fliers explaining our protest," she said with a worried look. "Maybe we should protest in front of the developer's office." Hannah jammed her earbuds back in. She thumbed through her phone and saw a video someone posted. "Hey, we *did* make the news!"

"How do we look? Tell me!" Hailey said, jumping up.

Hannah unplugged the earbuds so Hailey could hear. But as they watched their smiles were soon replaced by frowns. "We sounded like a couple of fifth-grade wackos."

"I should've said we're going into the *sixth* grade," Hailey said.

"I didn't mean that. You shouldn't have used fancy scientific names like *Thamnophis radix*. Why didn't you stick to the snake's common name?" Hannah asked.

"I was afraid that saying 'plains garter snake' sounded *too* common," Hailey replied.

"And you shouldn't have called the developer a greedy moneygrubber," Hannah added.

"*Now* you tell me," Hailey answered.

Hannah looked back at her phone. "Now they're interviewing a snake scientist," she told Hailey.

"Great!" Hailey said.

Hannah listened, shaking her head. "*Not* great— the scientist said there are millions of these garter snakes. He said they're no more endangered than mice."

Now Hailey was mad. "But that's not the point. This specific-particular-unique-special Snake Town is going to get wiped out," she said. "It gets cold in the winter around here. Where else can those hundreds and hundreds of snakes go?"

By now Hannah was playing a game. "They tried to interview the farmer who's selling the land to the developer," she told Hailey when she'd finished. "The farmer said he wasn't ready to talk to any radio station about snakes. Face it, Hailey—we're doomed." Hailey lowered her sign.

A faded red pickup stopped by the curb as the girls slumped together on the courthouse steps. A white-haired man in blue overalls climbed out and walked toward them. He said, "You the kids who want to save snakes?"

Hannah and Hailey looked over, surprised. "Yeah," Hailey said, her fists tightening. "What about it?"

"Don't you think making a place for people is more

important?" he said, hands on his hips.

Hannah stayed calm. "We have nothing against trailer parks, sir. We just don't want a trailer park where the snakes den."

The man's face was leathery brown below a white forehead. He stared at their sign.

"I thought that scientist said the snakes were pretty common around here," he replied.

"It's true that they're not endangered." Hannah tried to sound like a grownup. "But that area is a very special place for garter snakes. It has lots of rocky dens where the snakes can stay warm in the winter. When they gather there in fall, their bright orange backs look so beautiful."

"Orange?" The man's eyes looked hurt, as if the girls had bopped him over the head with their sign. "Are the snakes really *orange*?"

Hannah remembered not to sound stuffy. "Well, they're mostly brown, black, and yellow, but they have an orange stripe down their backs."

"An orange stripe?" The man's voice was soft, as if he were talking to himself. "I never did know where those stripey snakes lived. Never bothered looking, either. Man, oh man, I could never *stand* snakes." He walked back to his pickup. Then he yelled, "You kids might as well pack up your sign and go home."

Hailey's temper did the talking. "We're staying right here, mister!"

The man looked around, but he didn't seem mad. He just shook his head.

Hailey watched the faded red pickup disappear down the street. "Man, oh man," she said, imitating the man's voice. "Boy, is he out of it. Nobody talks like that anymore, do they?"

Hannah turned to Hailey. "I'm hot, and I'm hungry. How long are we going to stay out here? Come on, admit it, Hailey—we're done for. Nobody but us cares about those snakes."

"We have our lunches. We have water bottles. We have sun block. We just *have* to stay," Hailey declared.

Hannah jammed her earbuds in again. "Well, I think it's over," she said. "So I'm protesting under protest. But I guess I can stay until my battery dies."

The two girls took separate lunch breaks so one of them could always hold up the sign by the courthouse steps. They weren't talking to each other anyway. After lunch they paced slowly back and forth along the steps, looking as alone and hopeless as they felt.

At one o'clock, Hannah suddenly stopped. She stood stiff and still in the blazing

sun, staring intently at her phone. Then she yanked out her earbuds.

Hailey asked cautiously, "Did your battery die or something?"

"Let's go home." Hannah's smile seemed as wide as the street. She almost looked crazy, her smile was so big.

Hailey was worried about her friend. "Just take it easy," she said. "I'll get you inside where it's cool. You can drink some water. You can sit down. You'll be all right."

Hannah turned to Hailey and beamed. "The reporter finally interviewed the farmer who owns the land."

"So?" Hailey said slowly.

"He said his younger brother knew about a special place where there were hundreds of snakes. But the farmer would never go with

his brother. All he remembered was his brother saying snakes with an orange stripe on their backs denned along the river."

"I don't get it. What's his brother got to do with this?" Hailey asked.

"His brother was killed in the Iraq War," Hannah said. "The man said he would never sell his land along the river now that he knew his brother's favorite snakes lived there," she continued. "The farmer is going to give it to the city to keep as a nature preserve. He said because of his brother, he knew that some people could love snakes. But you know what else he told the reporter?"

Hailey shook her head. Hannah beamed a smile, and told her. "He said, 'Man, oh man, I could never *stand* snakes!'"

On the way home from the store the other day, I stopped to watch the pigeons in the park. One big pigeon kept strutting back and forth in front of the bench where I sat. He cocked a red eye at me and stared suspiciously.

Soon the warm sun and pleasant breeze began to make me feel sleepy. My eyelids got heavier and heavier. My head began to droop—down, down, and *zzzzzzz*.

In a dream I thought I heard a gruff voice say, *"Cccccooooo*, hiya, bud! I'm Big Ed. Got any garbage with you?"

"What's this?" I said. "A talking pigeon! Is that really *you* talking?"

"It had better be," cooed Big Ed. "Do you see anyone else around here?"

"OK, it's fine with me if you want to talk, but why do you want garbage?" I asked.

"Because I'm bored with bread crumbs!" Big Ed replied. "That's all you people ever think of giving us—bread crumbs. You know, we pigeons like a change once in a while. We can peck a meal out of almost anything."

"That's for sure," I said. "Who says you guys are pea-brains? You know, I think it's exciting the way you pigeons can do tricks in the air and have races and carry messages."

Big Ed stuck his beak in the air and sneered, "Hold it! We're not *that* kind of pigeon. We're street pigeons—we make it on our own. Those fancy pigeons that people raise have to live in special coops and be fed special food. They're our prissy cousins. *We* survive almost anywhere. And those pigeons that carry messages aren't too sharp anyway. They can only carry a message one way—from a distant place to their home coop. They can't take an answer back," he scoffed.

"Well, I've never seen them in action, but I've seen

pigeons like you all my life. Where did you come from?" I asked.

Big Ed struck a pose, cleared his throat and began, "We've been around since long before civilization began. Our ancestors were wild rock doves from Europe and Asia. Some of them still live on the sides of cliffs there. Now *we* live on man-made cliffs," he explained.

"Man-made cliffs?" I asked.

"Of course. What do you think all those tall buildings are? Say, are you *sure* you don't have anything to eat with you?" he asked.

I remembered that I did have some cheese crackers in my grocery bag, so I told him about them.

"Well, hand 'em over," he demanded. "At least they're better than stale bread."

I got out the box, then crumbled a few crackers and tossed them on the ground. Three nearby pigeons fluttered over to help themselves. Big Ed threatened them with some *ccccooooos*. Then he drove them off with flapping wings and hard pecks.

"Gotta show 'em who's boss," he explained.

While he nibbled on the cheese cracker crumbs I asked him, "How do you live on our man-made cliffs?"

"They have windowsills, ledges, air conditioners, overhangs, gutters, roof corners. You name it, and we can roost on it or build a nest there," he answered.

I suddenly realized that I

had never seen a pigeon nest, and said so.

Big Ed pecked at the last few cracker crumbs. He looked around cautiously, then came closer. "We build 'em where you can't get at 'em," he muttered out of the side of his beak. "There are a lot of you people who don't like us, you know."

"But in the city, where do you get enough grass to build your nests?" I wondered.

"Grass? Who needs it?" he cooed. "Sure, it comes in handy. But grass is for the birds. Give us a few sticks and some old rags or paper and we can pile up a fine nest."

"Well, your nests must work," I admitted. "There certainly are a lot of you around. You must raise *huge* families."

"Wrong!" he cooed loudly.

"My mate lays only two eggs at a time. That's all."

"Then where do so many of you come from?" I asked.

With a careful look to make sure no one else was listening, Big Ed explained. "My mate lays only two eggs at a time, but she does it several times a year."

"Aha!" I said. "So that's it. Do baby pigeons eat bread crumbs and potato chips too?"

"Of course not," he replied. "For the first week after they hatch my mate feeds them a special 'pigeon milk' that we can make in our *crop*. That's a special food storage sac in our throat. Pigeon fathers make 'pigeon milk' too. So I can help feed the youngsters while she is laying eggs in another nest for her next brood."

"Then you have families at any time of year, I suppose."

"Almost. The winter months are not as good for family raising—but sometimes we try anyway. After all, there can't be too many of us. We have to stay ahead of all the people who try to get rid of us. Some even try to poison us!"

"Well, Ed," I said, "not all of us hate pigeons. You pigeons are pretty to watch as you flutter around in the sunlight. But you sure do make an ugly mess with your droppings. Can't you do anything about that?"

"Sorry; as long as there are pigeons there will be pigeon droppings. We certainly can't do anything about *that*," he grumbled.

"No, I suppose you can't," I chuckled. "But your droppings can carry diseases. Pigeon droppings also eat away stone. Your droppings have damaged stone buildings and famous stone statues all over the world. Can't you perch somewhere else?"

"Ccccoooo, a perch is a perch," Big Ed replied. "Maybe *you* should stop building statues in *our* parks."

"Now, Ed, suppose we did that. We could take away the benches around the statues too. Then fewer people would come to the parks, and you know what that means— fewer handouts for you guys!"

Big Ed gave me a worried glance with his bright red eyes. "I'd better mention this at an important meeting we're having about a new statue being put up across town." Then he did a few flutters for me to remind me how pretty a pigeon can look in flight. When he came back, he cooed, "Gotta go now." As he flew away, he called back, "Thanks for the crackers!"

Suddenly a dog nearby began to bark. I woke up and thought about my dream. I smiled as I remembered Big Ed and his bluster.

Then I thought about all the thousands of dollars and hours people have spent trying to frighten pigeons away. Every big city has a pigeon problem, but nothing seems to get rid of them. *Maybe we should try to build pigeon-proof buildings where they can't roost,* I thought. But even if we did that, I knew there would still be plenty of pigeons around to watch. As Big Ed said, they sure do keep ahead of us.

# To the Rescue

## By Linda Rae Apolzon

When we got to the pond that Friday afternoon, summer sunshine was making the water sparkle. A blue jay screeched at us. Noah—he's my little brother—croaked at a frog.

Noah is only five, but he goes everywhere with me and my friend Jack. My mom started a business at home last summer. Now every day she says to me, "Zach, if you and Jack could just watch Noah, that would be ..."

"... a big help," I always answer. "I know. Come on, Noah."

It's a nice little pond, not deep or anything, so I'm allowed to go there without a grownup. That day, though, it wasn't so nice. Someone had left beer cans all over.

"Slobs," Jack mumbled, picking up cans.

I rinsed them in the water before putting them in my backpack, because I didn't want it to smell like beer. I was mad. I mean, it's not our pond—it belongs to the college where Dad teaches. But still.

I finished rinsing and stood up. Then I froze. "Jack," I said, "look at that duck."

Near the edge of the pond, a duck was swimming in circles. I could tell by his long, pointy tail feathers and long neck that he was a male pintail. He dipped his bill into the water, then tipped his head back and gulped. One ring of a plastic six-pack holder was around his neck. I wondered how the bird could swallow. Another ring was around one of his wings, keeping him from flying.

He was pretty close to me, so I dived for him. Unfortunately I don't get much practice tackling ducks. The pintail paddled away in panic. Noah watched and worried. "Zach, we're not allowed to swim in the pond," he said.

"Zach wasn't swimming," said Jack. "He was trying to catch that duck so we can get those plastic rings off. If we don't, the duck might starve or get caught by a predator."

Jack thought he could chase the pintail toward me if I stood as still as I could. Jack circled the pond, trying to direct the duck. Noah wiggled around. He kept giving us advice. "Ducks are fast, so you have to move *quick*."

"Quick, Noah. Right. Now, shhhhh!"

The duck drifted nearer to me. Jack splashed toward him from the opposite side of the pond. Noah jumped up and down on the muddy shore. I grabbed for the duck when he was close enough. The pin-

tail slipped away by jumping into the air, but then he plopped right back down again and swam away. By this time, Noah had fallen in the mud.

It went on like that all afternoon. Finally we gave up and trudged home. All three of us were wet and muddy and smelled like pond scum. Our parents weren't going to be happy.

I told Dad about the duck. He frowned. Then he said, "We need something to

catch him with. How about an old sheet?"

The next morning we—including Dad, who was all excited about the plan—headed for the pond. We took a sheet, scissors (for cutting the six-pack holder), and a bag of corn. When we threw some corn into the pond, ducks and geese charged at it.

"Now throw some on the shore," Dad said. A couple of mallards waddled up to eat the corn. So did our pintail.

Jack got more corn ready while Dad and I unfolded the sheet. Noah kept whispering "Shhhhh!" The pintail was right in front of us, next to the mallards. Dad and I raised the sheet.

"Quick!"

"Quack!"

We got him! Under the sheet, the duck flapped furiously. "Dad?" said Noah.

"Not now," Dad replied. We unwrapped our catch and found—a female mallard. Noah pointed to the pond. Bobbing on the water was our pintail. He eyed us suspiciously and kept his distance from us.

"That stinks," said Noah.

We spent the rest of the day there. All I can say is that the geese and ducks had a feast—except for our pintail. He was spooked and wouldn't come close. By the time we left, he was at the other end of the pond, not moving much. How long had he been tangled in those rings? How long would he be able to survive?

Next day there were thunderstorms, and Mom kept us home. On Monday Dad said he'd go with us after lunch. We got more corn ready.

I didn't know what we'd

find—if anything. Had the duck been caught and eaten? Even Noah was quiet as he, Jack, and I got near the pond. Then I stopped in my tracks.

There was our pintail with his back to us. He was nibbling at something on land. Dad had the sheet, but he was too far behind us to help. I looked at Jack, and he nodded. The two of us got between the duck and the water. I signaled, and we both rushed toward him.

All I saw were gray webbed feet and grabbing hands. Then we heard Noah screaming from the edge of the pond, "I got him! I got him!"

"Way to go, Noah!" Dad raced over and held the duck with the sheet while Jack got the scissors. I had never felt better than when cutting off that plastic holder.

The duck didn't even try to get loose—he was probably weak from hunger. We walked him to the water, set him down, and he slipped in. He swam around for a few minutes, just relaxing. Then he started dipping into the water and pulling up plants and stuff to eat.

I cut that six-pack holder into a zillion pieces and put every one of them in my backpack. Then Jack, Noah, and I sat down on the grass. Dad grinned at us.

Bright sunshine made the water sparkle. Noah croaked at a frog. Everything was back the way it should be.

# Gussie Goes Hunting

by Mary Mastin

Gussie was a garter snake. She was very pretty with her bright black eyes and three lemon-yellow stripes. One stripe ran straight down the center of her back. The same kind of bright line went down each of her sides to the tip of her tail, 24 inches (61 cm) from her head. In between the stripes, Gussie was dark and spotted.

Being a sensible snake, Gussie knew exactly what to do when spring began to warm the countryside. She crawled out of her winter den in the old rock pile and stretched out on her favorite log. Most of her days were spent dozing in the sun, and at night she went back to the rock pile.

After two weeks of sluggishly waking up, Gussie went to look for food and a summer home. She slid over the tree roots and through the dry leaves with only the slightest rustling sound. She was hunting for a fat little mouse, but they all seemed to be hiding where Gussie couldn't find them.

On she went to the edge of the woods and out into a small meadow. Softly she moved through the new grass, her forked tongue darting out ahead. She used it to feel her way and pick up the scent of food. As she pulled her tongue back, and touched the roof of her mouth with it, she caught a familiar smell. Only a few feet away was a thick clump of weeds and low bushes. She slipped through the rough stalks. She had found a bird's nest with eggs in it!

She pushed her face up over the nest's edge … right into another face! Gussie hissed a warning. Too late, she saw the pointed nose and beady little eyes of a weasel—one of her deadliest enemies. Yikes! She backed away so quickly that she looped over her own tail, nearly turning herself upside down. No eggs for breakfast this morning!

Gussie streaked across the meadow to hide in the weeds along the edge of the river. Soon her quick eyes saw the top of a blunt nose coming toward her. She tensed, ready to snatch the frog headfirst in her mouth. But it wasn't a frog; it was a bad-tempered old black snake with a huge appetite for young garter snakes. She turned tail and fled. She shot over a rock and under an old pine stump beside the river. She slid into a small hole only to find a pair of fiery eyes and a mouthful of snarling teeth that belonged to an unfriendly mink!

Whsst! Gussie backed out of the burrow and turned. Scrunch! The teeth closed on her tail. She tried to wriggle up over the stump, but one of the roots broke, sending her and the mink into the river.

Gussie was free, but still frightened.

She swam upstream until she came to a small sandy bay. Now tired, she began to float toward the shore. She found herself in the middle of a school of minnows. They were so scared and confused that they swam right into her mouth!

After gobbling her breakfast, Gussie wriggled up on the beach to hide under a large boulder. There were no weasels, black snakes, or minks to threaten her here—but plenty of fish.

Any sensible snake would spend the summer there, and that's just what Gussie did!

# SCREAMS & WHISPERS
## BY JUDY BRAUS

Ryan hurried down the street in his lizard costume. Tonight was his nature club's Halloween party! He turned in at his friend Ethan's house and knocked on the door.

"Hi, Ryan! Wow, you look awesome!" Ethan exclaimed as he opened the door.

"Thanks," said Ethan, "but keeping up with a spider's eight legs isn't easy."

"I can't wait to see Mr. Elliott's costume. And Emma said she was coming as a jellyfish or a bat," said Ryan as he adjusted his mask.

"Don't we make a great pair—a lizard and a spider," chuckled Ethan. "You know, this will be the first time I've seen the old house Mr. Elliott bought."

"Same here," answered Ryan. "My sister said people think his house is

haunted. Some weird old lady used to live there, and they say her ghost makes strange noises at night."

"Nah, there are no such things as ghosts," said Ethan as the boys started off down the street.

"Anyway, from now on all our nature club meetings will be at Mr. Elliott's. So maybe we'll get a chance to find out."

"Anyway," said Ryan, "It's getting dark ... we'd better hurry."

When the boys got there, they knocked on the door, and Mr. Elliott opened it.

"*Eek!*" he screamed, pretending to be scared. Then he laughed. "Great costumes, boys! Come on in. We have lots to do before the rest of the gang gets here."

As Ryan and Ethan stepped inside they heard a

loud crash on the side of the house.

"What's that?" Ryan asked.

"Oh, it's just one of the shutters blowing in the wind. Since I've only been here a week, I still have a lot to fix up," answered Mr. Elliott.

Ryan and Ethan took off their masks and looked around the old house. In the dim light they could see shabby old furniture and faded wallpaper that was cracked and peeling. The place really looked lousy!

"Wow, it *does* look haunted," whispered Ryan.

"Yeah," said Ethan. "It's *spooky.*"

"Come on, you guys," said Mr. Elliott. "There are black and orange streamers and some Jack-o'-lanterns to put up. Here's the tape. I'm off to the store to get cider and some apples for bobbing."

As Mr. Elliott walked out, Ryan noticed the full moon shining outside.

"Look, Ethan, it's a perfect night for vampires. There's the full moon."

"Not vampires, Ryan. It's werewolves that come out and howl when the moon is full."

"Come on, we've got to start decorating. Let's put the streamers here in the living room," said Ryan. "Hey—did you hear that?"

"Hear what?" asked Ethan.

"That ticking sound," Ryan answered. "Shhhhh … listen."

Ethan could just barely hear a slight *tick, tick, tick,* coming from the other side of the room.

"It's probably just an old clock," Ethan said, shrugging his shoulders. He looked around. There was no clock in the room.

Then, just as suddenly as it had started, the ticking stopped.

Someone knocked on the

door. Ryan ran to open it. Standing on the porch was a huge vampire bat. Ryan gulped.

"Hi, Ryan," the bat said. "How do you like my costume? Gruesome, huh?"

"Is that you, Emma?" Ryan asked.

"Who did you think it was, silly?" laughed Emma, closing the door.

"Gosh, what a-creepy house," said Emma, looking around.

"Ryan, Emma, come here—quick!" Ethan called from the living room.

"What's wrong?" asked Ryan.

"Voices," whispered Ethan. "Here, behind this wall. Listen."

"Oh, come on, Ethan—voices?" scoffed Emma. "How can people be talking behind a wall?"

Suddenly the ticking started again.

"What's that?" asked Emma. "It sounds kind of like a time bomb."

"We don't know what it is," said Ryan. "It keeps starting and stopping. This place is giving me the creeps."

"Aw, you guys, this is silly," said Emma.

"Maybe the old lady's ghost really *is* here," said Ryan with a shiver.

Just as he said that, the wind made a loud, moaning noise through a crack in a window. The kids moved closer to each other. Suddenly a scream filled the room. Everyone jumped.

"What was *that?*" whispered Ryan.

"It came from somewhere upstairs," Emma said.

"Let's see what's up there," said Ethan.

"I wouldn't go up there if you paid me!" said Ryan. "Let's get out of here."

"Oh, it's probably just the wind," said Ethan, hoping it was true.

"The *wind* doesn't scream, Ethan," said Emma.

"Come on, let's just go see," urged Ethan.

Suddenly another loud screech rang out.

"I'm getting out of here!" shouted Ryan. "This place really *is* haunted."

Ethan and Emma were scared, too, but they stopped Ryan from leaving.

"Listen, let's get these decorations up and wait for Mr. Elliott," said Ethan calmly. "He should be back any minute."

"Well," said Ryan, "OK, but let's all stick together until he gets here."

"So you really think the old lady is haunting this place?" asked Emma, hanging up a streamer.

"Who else would have screamed?" said Ryan.

Just then there was another scream. All three club members stopped what they were doing; their hearts thumped in their chests.

"It's the old lady again," whispered Ryan. "Let's get out of here!" he added, heading for the door.

But just then Mr. Elliott walked in.

"What's going on?" he called.

"There are ghosts in here!" said Ryan, breathing quickly. "The old lady's screaming and, and, we're scared!"

"Tell him about the ticking," said Emma.

Mr. Elliott shook his head. "Wait a minute. Slow down and tell me what's happened."

"Well, we heard all these weird sounds: ticking but there's no clock, people whispering behind a wall, and just now screams upstairs," Ryan explained.

"Aren't you exaggerating?" Mr. Elliott smiled.

"Show him where the ticking and voices were,

Ethan," said Emma.

"Behind that wall," said Ryan, pointing.

Mr. Elliott leaned over and listened. The wallpaper had peeled away from the corner, and there was a crack in the wall. Mr. Elliott chuckled. "Do you remember what we talked about at our last club meeting?" he asked.

"Umm—honeybees," remembered Ethan. "We were talking about how they survive the winter. But what does that have to do with us and this haunted house?"

"That's what's living in this wall. The bees have made their hive inside, and there must be a hole to the outside so they can fly in and out. But in the winter, they stay huddled up together to keep warm. The noise is just their wings buzzing as they move back and forth.

"Now, let's go up to the attic and find the mysterious screamer," he said with a smile. "Let me get a flashlight."

They all followed Mr. Elliott up the creaky stairs. Mr. Elliott shined his light just as a huge owl flew out the broken attic window.

"It's a barn owl," he shouted, "and it's a beauty! That's your screamer, kids."

Ethan looked at Ryan and Emma and started to laugh. "I guess we were pretty silly," he said with an

embarrassed smile.

"Wait a minute. How about the ticking?" asked Ryan.

"Let's go find out," said Mr. Elliott.

When they were back in the living room, Ethan pointed to an old rocking chair. "The ticking seemed to come from near that rocker."

Mr. Elliott looked around the chair. "See these piles of sawdust on the floor?" he asked. "I'll bet if you were to sit in that old rocker, it might just fall apart.

"How come?" asked Emma.

"Tiny insects called death-watch beetles are boring through the wood and eating it. As they crawl, they make a ticking sound. It's just their hard shells knocking against the wood in the rocker."

He pulled off a piece of the rotting wood from the back of the chair. It was dry and crumbly.

"Look," he pointed. In his hand were a few tiny brown beetles. "Here they are! Now do you still think my house is haunted?" asked Mr. Elliott.

"I just hope the owl, the beetles, and the bees trick the others when they get here! But let's not tell them, and see what happens," said Emma as she bit into a big red apple.

# DESERT DANGER

BY ROBERT F. GRAY

Zerda the fennec (FEN-nick) slept safely in his burrow, coiled into a fluffy, sand-colored ball. His home in the hot lands of North Africa can be a harsh place to live. To avoid the worst heat, he and many other animals sleep during the day. At sundown he woke up—hungry and thirsty— and scurried to the burrow's entrance.

Zerda sniffed the air for danger. He studied each bush and listened for enemies, turning his large ears this way and that to pick up any warning sounds. Satisfied that he was safe, he darted to a water hole where other fennecs were drinking.

Now it was time to hunt. Zerda trotted briskly along the desert's hollows and ravines, nose to the ground, ears alert. Suddenly a skink (lizard) darted in front of him. Zerda leaped for it and, after a short chase, caught the lizard. He ate it and two large beetles. Then he went into an orchard to eat figs that had fallen from the trees. Just before dawn, he caught a mouse. But

because he was full he dug a hole in the sand, dropped the mouse into it, then replaced the sand with fast, sideward pats of his muzzle. That mouse would be good some other time.

With his future meal safe, the fox turned homeward. It was then that Aureus (AWR-ee-us) the jackal saw him. Aureus had not eaten for three nights, and at the sight of the tiny fox he set off in pursuit. In half a dozen leaps he caught and pinned Zerda. The terrified fox rolled over in the sand, kicking and biting. He caught the jackal by his nose and Aureus jumped back suddenly. Zerda streaked away—twisting and backtracking—trying to lose the long-legged jackal. But the race was uneven and Aureus closed the gap between them.

Zerda stopped running and began to dig madly in the soft sand. His forelegs threw the sand aside so rapidly that he seemed to be diving into the earth. When Aureus reached the spot, Zerda was deep beneath the surface. The jackal tried to unearth him, but Zerda stayed well out of reach, and the jackal gave up and slunk away.

Zerda stayed still beneath the sand. Only after the sun rose did he dig to the surface and stick his pointed muzzle out of the sand. He smelled no danger. He poked his head out. He neither saw nor heard an enemy. So he wriggled from his hole and raced homeward. He scurried along the tunnels that connected his burrow with those of other fennecs. Reaching his own neat, grass-lined den, he flopped down, curled himself into a fluffy ball, and fell asleep. It had been quite a day, and tomorrow would be another for the tiny desert fox.

Note: The fennec's scientific name is *Fennecus zerda*. The desert (or common) jackal's name is *Canis aureus*.

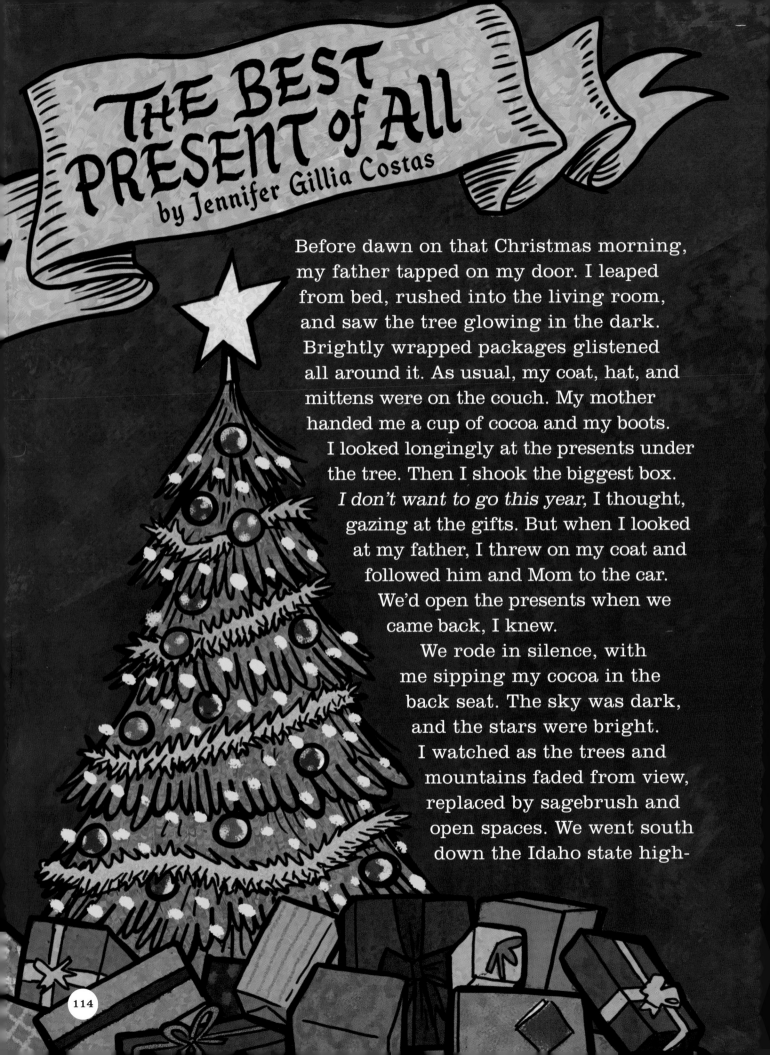

# THE BEST PRESENT of All
## by Jennifer Gillia Costas

Before dawn on that Christmas morning, my father tapped on my door. I leaped from bed, rushed into the living room, and saw the tree glowing in the dark. Brightly wrapped packages glistened all around it. As usual, my coat, hat, and mittens were on the couch. My mother handed me a cup of cocoa and my boots. I looked longingly at the presents under the tree. Then I shook the biggest box. *I don't want to go this year*, I thought, gazing at the gifts. But when I looked at my father, I threw on my coat and followed him and Mom to the car. We'd open the presents when we came back, I knew.

We rode in silence, with me sipping my cocoa in the back seat. The sky was dark, and the stars were bright. I watched as the trees and mountains faded from view, replaced by sagebrush and open spaces. We went south down the Idaho state highway through a tiny desert town and finally onto a private dirt road. My father's old friend Hal owned this huge piece of land in the middle of the desert. Hal had found springs on the land that helped form a desert wetland. He bought it and made it into a bird refuge.

"I keep the place just for the birds," Hal told my father back then, "but you and your family can visit it whenever you like. I know you'll respect it." He gave my dad the only other set of keys for the gate to his land.

We came to Hal's land just once a year, on Christmas morning. "Some things are so special that, if you did them every day, you'd ruin them for sure," my father said.

Finally we parked at the edge of the refuge. I gazed up at the star-filled sky with its slice of moon. On the path in front of us, ten quails scurried away. They looked like busy old ladies. Their feather "bonnets" perched over their heads.

We walked toward the springs along the dry path. The cold, sandy soil crunched under our feet. Then we saw the marshy ponds fed by the springs. A hint of daylight in the eastern sky allowed us to see the dark shapes of birds nearby.

When we came to our spot between the springs, an explosive sound startled us. It was hundreds of mallards rising from the ponds at once. Beads of water hit my face. We stood as still as we could until they stopped circling overhead and settled back onto the ponds. Then we sat near the sagebrush and waited together in silence.

I noticed pinkness on the edge of the sky that comes just before sunrise. The pinkness spread as I watched.

A bald eagle circled the sky, then landed on a dead branch above us. It combed

its feathers with its
beak. Then it puffed
up just for a second before
shooting down to the water.
It rose with a fish in its feet and
faded into the pink, glowing sky
above us.

A great blue heron flapped
lazily over us. Several small
diving ducks sat on the
water. Then they sliced

into the water, diving for food.
Their speed shocked me. I held my
breath. Before I could let it out, I was
startled by the rattling sound of a king-
fisher. The bird darted about and dived
into the water, bringing up a little fish.
After that, all was still.

I could hear the distant sound
of honking. I leaned toward
it. Specks of black pep-
pered the sky. Then,
like a huge
wave, a

flock of geese flowed in. In V patterns, check marks, and lines, they filled the sky. Time stood still as they washed over us.

"Thank you, thank you, thank you," I heard my dad whisper.

"Merry Christmas," my mom said as she kissed his cheek. I just watched the geese and thought about the holiday.

The light of the new day shone behind the geese. Everything brightened as the geese dropped from the sky. And as they settled in among the mallards on the ponds, all became still again.

We watched for a while as the ducks

and geese paddled around.
A few geese waddled onto the
land. Everything was so peaceful
and quiet and just right.

Finally, we turned to walk to our car. I
found a goose feather and held on to it.

Even today, many years later, these two
things still give me a Christmas feeling:
the sight of beautiful big geese filling the
sky and the sound of their honking cries
that seem to hush everything below.

# THE FLAMELIGHTS OF OOLUMAREE

"by Bonnie Bisbee"

Oora was green and scaly, and she had a long tail. But the United Planets Council put her in my class of humans at school. She learned our language, Earth-ish, pretty well. And she caught on to most of our lessons and games.

But many of the human kids thought that an ammu like her was strange. Some of them called Oora "Lizard Lips." And we were living on *her* world!

I had come to this planet, Oolumaree, with my parents just a couple of months ago. They were part of a Universal Minerals scouting team. Huge dinosaurs used to live on Oolumaree millions of years ago, they'd all died out. All except one type of small, gentle dinosaur— the ammu. Ammus walked upright and developed a big brain.

Like my friend Oora!

After school one day, Oora said, "I show you ammus' secret treasure?"

"Sure!" I replied.

I followed her through the forest, wondering what kind of treasure the ammus might have. The forest looked very different from forests on Earth. Some trees had pink leaves, like puffs of cotton candy. And the planet's twin suns gave everything two shadows.

Finally we came to a huge rock cliff with a misty waterfall cascad-

ing down it. Oora led me along a narrow passage behind the waterfall. Inside was a cave. It was lit up by hundreds of glowing stones! Each flashed a different color: ruby red, purple, aqua blue, or gold. "Lovely!" I whispered.

Oora's long tail twitched nervously. "*Maramoos*—flamelights," she said in a hushed, whispering voice.

Just then we heard voices. I figured that we weren't supposed to be in here. Sure enough, Oora pulled me back into the shadows. We crouched down behind a rock.

We peeked out and saw a man and a woman coming toward us. Their uniforms showed that they were two Universal Minerals scouts. One of them whistled at the sight of the glowing stones. "This cave must have formed them somehow," he said.

"We could make a fortune selling these gems on other planets!" the woman said. Then she frowned. "But what will the ammus say if we take them?"

"Don't worry about them—the ammus will be declared Nonpersons at tomorrow's team meeting," the man said. "After all, they're not like us. They live in the forest like animals. They don't even use fire or build any shelters. So they shouldn't have rights like people. And they won't be allowed to own any mineral rights on Oolumaree."

"Then Universal Minerals will claim the rights to all these sparklies," the woman said, smiling, "and we'll be rewarded for finding them!"

Finally they left. Oora didn't talk as she walked me home. Her blue eyes looked worried. At my family's living unit, she said: "If humans take away flamelights, ammus will die!"

I gasped. What could this mean? I sure didn't want anyone to hurt Oora and other ammus. "Let's tell Jamar," I suggested. "She's the head of the United Planets Council here. If anyone can stop the Universal Minerals company, she could. I'll go with you tomorrow."

"Thanks, Yuki!" Oora's scaly lips looked like they were smiling. "See you tomorrow, then!" She disappeared into the forest.

Three months later Oora and I waited in the forest

near the big rock cliff, along with other humans and ammus. It was dark. The waterfall tumbled softly.

We were waiting for a "surprise" the ammus said was coming. They said it would prove to us humans that the ammus needed the flamelights. "This had better be good," I whispered to Oora, "or the humans will start taking the flamelights. I don't think most people believe that you ammus depend on the glowing stones."

Oora stood stiffly beside me. "Surprise is good," she said. Oolumaree's three moons came up, full and bright. The last moon's purple rays cast a magical light on the woodland scene. We were the first humans to see Oolumaree's Triple Fullmoon Night.

Suddenly something started moving. From behind the waterfall crawled thou-sands of flashing "stones." Spilling out into the forest, they looked like a sparkling river of fire. Then the "stones" sprouted wings and flew off among the trees!

"So the maramoos are really creatures!" Jamar said, smiling.

Spokesperson Rumanoo nodded. His big red crest made him look very important. "Soon we show you ammu city inside rock cliff," he said. "We ammus have carved many caves in the cliff for our homes and shops. But every year we leave them. For a time we live simply in forest. Young maramoos crawl into our quiet, dark caves. They turn hard and still—like glowing stones.

"On Triple Fullmoon Night, maramoos awake as adults, and they fly back to forest. We ammus return to caves. Then maramoos make wonderful food in forest,

sweet and thick."

"Like honey!" I said out loud. Jamar nodded at me and put her finger to her lips.

"Maramoos give us food. Is all we eat for many months. Maramoos help us; we help maramoos. For ages, it has been this way," he said.

For a while we watched the little living lights as they flitted through the woods all around us. Finally Jamar said, "I guess those glowing 'stones' would be hard to catch now!" Everyone laughed.

She went on: "This surprise should remind us to be careful before we take natural things from any world. Remember the hard lessons we learned back on Earth about upsetting the balance of life." She turned to spokesperson Rumanoo. "You ammus should decide what is best for you and the flamelights; we humans should not interfere," she said firmly.

No one argued about her decision, though some scouts looked disappointed.

Then Rumanoo spoke up. "Oolumaree can spare some real glowing stones. We show you. We use them to light up our cave city. Have other useful minerals too. Here is deal—we give you some

stones and minerals. You help us reach stars. Good deal?"

"Good!" said the team leader from Universal Minerals. Jamar nodded.

While the grownups went on talking, we kids—ammus and human—invented a new game called "Three Shadow Tag."

And nobody ever called Oora "Lizard Lips" again!

we jump in puddles

An imprint of The Rowman & Littlefield Publishing Group, Inc.
MuddyBootsBooks.com
Distributed by
NATIONAL BOOK NETWORK
800-462-6420

For more fun go to **www.RangerRick.com**